Quest

Quest

Marcia Zina Mager

Illustrations by Travis Weaver

MAMAKI PRESS

HONOLULU, HI

Published in the United States by Mamaki Press.

ISBN: 979-8-9863945-0-3
ISBN: 979-8-9863945-1-0 (Hardcover)
ISBN: 979-8-9863945-2-7 (Ebook)

For bulk purchase and for booking, contact:

marciazinamager@gmail.com
www.marciazinamager.com

Summary: An unhappy middle-aged bachelor from New York City reluctantly embarks on an otherworldly adventure in Ireland where he must face his vulnerabilities, and discovers a new way of seeing Nature and the world.
Suggested Categories: Parable, Myth, Fable—Fiction. Magic, Fantasy, Adventure, Fairies, Fairytales— Fiction. Self-actualization, Self-help—Psychology. Central Park, New York City, Ireland —Fiction. Spirituality, Nature, Ecology,

Library of Congress Control Number: 2022908146

Cover art, title page art and *Quest* pin art on p.215:
Barbara Mckell (www.barbaramckell.com)
Interior Illustrations by Travis Weaver (www.travisweaver.org)
Cover & book design by Sheila Smallwood (www.sheilasmallwooddesign.com)

FIRST EDITION

Dedicated to the Divine Tenderness
Within Us All

"*When the animals come to us,*
asking for our help,
will we know what they are saying?
When the plants speak to us
in their delicate, beautiful language,
will we be able to answer them?
When the planet herself
sings to us in our dreams,
will we be able to wake ourselves,
and act?"

—Gary Lawless

The Journey

Prologue

I<small>T WAS A QUIET</small> S<small>UNDAY</small> in March when the ancient forest emerged, like a phantom, out of the mist.

The little girl and her grandmother left their cottage just after sunrise, as they always did on Sundays, and headed to church. The cold and rainy weather, typical for Ireland this time of year, forced them to bundle in extra sweaters and shawls. They walked the same road as always, the one that wound its way past sleepy stone cottages where tea brewed in copper kettles and peat fires smoldered in stone hearths. The little girl and her grandmother walked silently, hand in hand, through the damp, gray morning.

Beyond the wet, rugged landscape, past acres of rolling

meadows, the massive stand of towering trees rose, like giant warriors, piercing the steel sky—pines and cedars, yew and ash, oak and beech tangled within each other's shadows, their scents sweet and pungent. This was an old, old forest, imbued with hidden life and mystery.

Deep within the wooded recesses, and deeper still within a grove of giant yew trees older than time itself, a strange fire burned. Slender white flames leapt and danced in a perfect circle. And what appeared to lay in the center of the circle was a thick pile of leaves, bark, and twigs. Yet a closer look revealed no random heap of forest debris. What lay within the ring of fire was a book. A book unlike any other on earth.

The book's form was like an old-world atlas, the kind displayed in glass cases of musty marble libraries. But the cover of this book was not made of hand tooled leather, its pages were not handsewn. This cover, made of thick coarse bark, the pages inside, a pale gold, torn from a papyrus tree, curled at the edges. The spine, woven of twigs and pine needles, was held together by sticky lumps of amber sap. This primitive design should not have worked, yet it did.

From the perimeter of the circle the book appeared to be moving, ever so slightly, its body swelling and flattening like a human breast, breathing, as if it were alive. And indeed, it was. Across the heavy bark cover crawled lines of red and black ants, shiny beetles, speckled ladybugs, iridescent dragonflies, and other creatures far too small to see. Within the weathered pages nestled spiders and tiny worms. To these creatures, this was not a book, it was a sentient, nurturing source, teeming with primordial wisdom, a sanctuary, a shelter as natural and real as the forest floor.

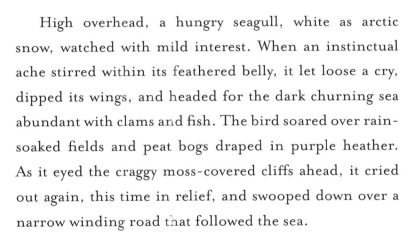

High overhead, a hungry seagull, white as arctic snow, watched with mild interest. When an instinctual ache stirred within its feathered belly, it let loose a cry, dipped its wings, and headed for the dark churning sea abundant with clams and fish. The bird soared over rain-soaked fields and peat bogs draped in purple heather. As it eyed the craggy moss-covered cliffs ahead, it cried out again, this time in relief, and swooped down over a narrow winding road that followed the sea.

The little girl noticed the bird right away. She was excited because today was her sixth birthday and of all the birds in Ireland seagulls were her favorite. She slowed her pace, pulling on her grandmother's hand. They had been walking for nearly an hour now and the old woman was tired. Grateful for the rest, her grandmother stopped and leaned against the low stone wall that bordered the blacktop road for miles. Nearly eighty-seven years old, she prided herself on her good health and keen eyesight. She could still cook and clean for a houseful and spot her cows a quarter of a mile away.

The little girl cried out, pointing toward the distant wetlands. "Grandmother, look! A forest! A giant forest!" The old woman lifted her eyes in the direction of her granddaughter's small, gloved hand and narrowed her gaze. She shivered, turning up her worn woolen collar and muttered a quick prayer that she would live to see another spring. Then she adjusted the frayed shawl that lay neatly across the shoulders of her coat. Tenderly, she patted her granddaughter. "Ah, 'tis a wild imagination you have, child," she sang in a lilting Irish brogue. "Surely there hasn't been a forest growin' there for more than two hundred years…"

PART ONE

Invitation

"We have been waiting for You.
You who hold these pages in your hands.
The time has come.
Do not be afraid.
You are the Chosen One."

—The Ancient Book of Fae

I

*"The best and most beautiful things in the world
cannot be seen or even touched.
They must be felt with the heart."*
—Helen Keller

LEPRECHAUNS PRANCED UP Fifth Avenue. Dozens of them. Brass marching bands followed, playing *Danny Boy* as thousands of rosy-cheeked onlookers sang along, braving the spring chill.

Saint Patrick's Day Parade in Manhattan was a loud, happy extravaganza. Families bundled in lime ski coats with matching earmuffs. College students waving shamrock green bagels, carrying Styrofoam pots of gold. An ocean of green as far as the eye could see. Bag pipe music filled the air and absolutely everyone seemed to be in an upbeat, festive mood.

Everyone except Alan Quinn Fitzpatrick.

Hunched on a bar stool at the upscale Cafe Emerald

Isle, recently opened on Fifth and 52nd Street, elbows pressed against the polished wood and brass bar, he sipped a steaming mug of coffee laced with too much Irish whiskey. So far, the day sucked. He overslept, nicked his chin shaving, and broke a dish rushing out of the apartment to meet Sheila for their five-month anniversary. But, as usual, he was late. When he arrived, she was gone.

On the counter beside him a large manila envelope, stuffed with a 278-page manuscript, stared up at him. It seemed to take up the full length of the bar, eclipsing the glass mug, New York Times, even his leather briefcase. Miserably, he stared back.

Why the hell had he brought it with him? Did he really think this time it would be different? Words of reassurance? An offer to publish? Who was he kidding? Year after year, always the same response. "Thank you for your recent submission. However..."

Twenty years he'd been writing, story after story, novel after novel. Girlfriends encouraging him. "You're good, Allan." Even agents thought he had talent. So out would come the next attempt, the desperate belief that this manuscript would be different. Then the inevitable rejection. And soon his file cabinets were stuffed with manila envelopes sheltering decades of broken dreams.

Finishing the coffee, he ordered a shot of whiskey. The bartender, a friendly young man with long blonde hair tied back in a neat ponytail eyed him sadly. "A bit early, don't you think, Mr. Fitzpatrick?"

Allan shrugged. He downed the shot in one gulp and started coughing. Truthfully, he hated whiskey. That's what made his newfound friendship with drinking even more pathetically tragic. An almost-alcoholic not only destroying himself with liquor, but with distaste as well.

"Happy Saint Paddy's Day!" a pretty, teenage girl called out as she walked by the open door, cheeks smudged with green. "May the luck of the Irish be with you forever!"

"Horseshit," he mumbled. For a guy fifty-percent Irish his luck seemed to be a hundred-percent crappy. Maybe that was because the other half of him was Jewish, on his father's side. At family gatherings they used to joke, "What do you get when you cross an Irishman with a Jew? A fighter who complains a lot."

About to order another shot, he glanced at his watch and decided against it. He had to go to the office, and they'd probably smell him a mile away. Tossing a twenty dollar bill on the counter, he headed out.

Fifth Avenue was packed even though the parade had ended an hour ago. As he started walking away the bartender came running, waving the envelope. "Keep it," Allan said bitterly. "Use it as a doorstop."

A group of young men, wearing black cardboard leprechaun hats, pushed past him, heading into the bar. He turned up his collar against the cold wind and before attempting to cross the crowded avenue, peered at his reflection in a storefront window.

At forty-three, most woman considered him extremely appealing. Though not tall enough for his own liking—five foot ten inches in his bare feet—he was pleased with how he looked, slender and fit. He had always been active, running marathons, playing tennis, or bicycle racing. His eyes, an endless blue, were the kind women noticed as soon as he entered a room, his hair, always a bit disheveled, thick dark brown, with distinctive streaks of gray. Yet it wasn't his looks or physique that ultimately drew women to him. There was something else, an aura, an invisible quality, something every woman wanted to touch, to liberate, whether they were conscious of it or not—a depth of tenderness and sensitivity he refused to acknowledge. While he appeared to be a successful bachelor with a steady stream of beautiful women who fell for him, he could never reciprocate. Through all the years of relationships, he'd never really loved anyone. In fact, the whole notion of love at first sight or falling in love seemed ludicrous. Whenever any woman started to get too close, whenever there seemed to be the possibility of true connection, something deep inside him recoiled, retreated, and the relationship inevitably fell apart.

Halfway across Fifth Avenue, he came to an abrupt halt. There must have been a hundred people blocking him from reaching the other side. He was so focused trying to jostle his way through the mob that he didn't feel the first two tugs on his pant leg. By the third tug, he looked down. The little girl staring up at him could not have been more than four or five years old, dressed in a homemade costume that made her look cuter that she already was. Poking out of the tousled mass of curly red hair were two silver pipe cleaners, an attempt, Allan mused, at some sort of insect antennae. Tied behind her pink ski jacket were a pair of wire framed wings draped in a gauzy pink material that shimmered. She wore pink tights that bagged at the knees and neon pink sneakers. In her right hand she clutched a drooping wand made of aluminum foil, cardboard, and glitter, her left-hand busy tugging at Allan's pant leg. Surprised and amused, he just stared.

"Hello," the little girl chirped.

"Well...hello to you too."

They looked at each other for a moment. Then the little girl said, in a very matter-of-fact tone of voice, "I need help." Allan glanced around the crowd for the child's parents.

"Are you lost?"

The little girl shook her head vigorously from side to side, indicating a definite no. Again, Allan scanned the crowd. No one seemed the least bit interested in them. "Then where's your mommy and daddy?" The little girl's eyes filled with tears. She bit down hard on her lower lip and would not let go of Allan's leg. "Do you see them anywhere?" Bravely, she turned her head to the right and to the left. Then she looked up at him, her lower lip quivering. She shook her head no. Allan knelt beside her. "Don't worry," he said, gently, taking her hand. "I promise, your parents will be right back."

Down at her level, with adults looming above, Allan felt like a child himself. He strained his neck looking everywhere for a distraught mother or father. In the dark hollow of the crowd, it was as if he and the little girl were invisible. Not knowing what else to do, he smiled. "I'm a fairy princess," she blurted out in an odd mixture of grief and enthusiasm.

"I see that," he said, and playfully touched one of her antennae. "You're very pretty."

She beamed. "My friend Tommy is a lepkon. He's green."

Allan smiled again. "A leprechaun," he said, enunciating slowly, realizing too late how ridiculous it was to be correcting a lost child. "But you didn't want to be a leprechaun, huh?"

She waved her droopy wand decisively. "Lepkons are fignewtins!"

"Fignewtins?" he repeated, puzzled.

She nodded eagerly. "Fignewtins of magination!"

"Fignewtins of..." He burst out laughing. "Oh, figments of imagination! Is that it?"

She nodded again, her expression quite serious.

"And fairies?" Allan asked, grinning.

She whispered, "Fairies are real," and her eyes shone with a conviction that made him uneasy.

An auburn-haired woman pushed through the crowd, nearly falling on top of them. "Annie!" she cried. "There you are! Thank God!" Like a true sprite, the little girl tumbled into her mother's arms. Mother and daughter burst into tears simultaneously.

"That man..." the little girl whimpered, pointing to Allan, "He promised you would come."

The young mother looked down at Allan, who was still kneeling, and smiled gratefully. "Thank you so much." Allan leapt to his feet, embarrassed.

The little girl hugged her mother tighter. "He saved me."

Allan laughed. "Well, I wouldn't go that far. You were pretty brave yourself." They beamed at him.

"Thank you again," she said, clutching her child. "I really don't know what I would have—"

"Well, never mind that," Allan offered. He touched her shoulder in a gesture of comfort. "Just enjoy the rest of the day." His spirits lifted, watching them disappear into the crowd. Maybe today wouldn't be so bad after all.

When he reached Central Park's busy entrance at Fifty-ninth street, the crowd had thinned. Joggers weaved in and out, mothers pushed baby carriages, a few homeless men begged for change, and a pair of teenage girls in green leather jackets, sat listlessly on a stone wall hunched over cell phones. Once inside, he headed down the wide walkway brimming with people, bordered on both sides by wooden and concrete benches and elm trees. Ignoring the crowd, he studied the labyrinth of bare branches overhead, his body relaxing with every step. Despite the cold, he could feel the beginning of spring. Soon enough the park's cherry trees and magnolias would be dripping in blossoms, daffodils and crocuses poking up between dead leaves and tree roots.

What was it about this place, he wondered as he strolled? Any time he ever seriously considered moving away, out of the city, he'd hesitate. He couldn't fathom leaving the park behind, like he had some kind of an intimate relationship with it, like it was the only one that could endure his moodiness. This was where he came when Marjorie dumped him. When Eve walked out. Whenever Sheila threatened to leave. He felt ashamed to admit how much he loved the park. "More than me," Sheila complained recently, after one of his long, late-evening jogs. Beyond the park's refuge, his life felt empty. No matter who he was with or what he was doing, a vague unhappiness haunted him, sometimes waking him in the middle of the night. Maybe that's why he wrote, story after story, seeking an insight or answer he could never seem to find.

A great white egret startled him, taking flight right above his head, into the crystalline blue sky. Looking around at the trees, at the mottled sparrows and red-headed cardinals darting among the branches, he knew Sheila was right. No matter how bad things got in his life, the park was always there to comfort him. He couldn't ignore how much better he felt whenever he entered, inhaled the fresh air, walked along the lake, or sat beneath a spectacular maple.

He thought about his crazy theory that he never dared tell anyone. That perhaps something else existed in nature, a hidden power that could some-how impact, even potentially transform human beings. His rational mind scoffed at the notion, rejecting it as a ridiculous childish concept. Sweeping his gaze toward the grove of elms, he reminded himself again, they're just trees, no matter how lovely, just an organic collection of leaves, roots, bark, and branches. Sure, they provide oxygen, absorb pollutants, cool the air. But they're just trees. An absurd idea to think they could ever be anything more.

Turning down a familiar dirt path to avoid the flow of people, he discovered an empty wooden bench nestled beneath a pair of gnarled elms. Nobody else around, he sat, closed his eyes, and let out a loud, clumsy "ahhhh." The day's disappointments spilled down his body, like rain. When he opened his eyes, he spotted, about twenty feet away, the creature.

At first, he thought it was a butterfly, the way it lay there, wings fluttering, so small and delicate. Was it wounded? Concerned, afraid someone could accidently crush it, he walked over. When he reached the patch of grass where it lay, he knelt, gently scooping it up with both hands. He wanted to move it to a more protected spot. As he stood up, he noticed something odd. To get a better view, he lifted his cupped hands closer to his face. And let out a scream.

He flung the creature to the ground. "What the hell?!" Had he seen what he thought he saw? Was he hallucinating? Stumbling back, he glanced around to see if anyone was nearby. Touching his chest, trying to calm himself, could the drinking have already affected his brain? He blinked a few times. "It can't be." He had to be sure.

His legs wouldn't budge. That's when he realized he was absolutely terrified.

He stared at the spot where he tossed it. The creature lay there, motionless. Finally he took a step. Then another. And another. Carefully, squatting down, sweat dripping from his forehead, breathing strained, he forced himself to look. His eyes widened in utter disbelief. Because there she was: a tiny, tiny woman, the size of his thumb, with golden white wings, sitting on a patch of Central Park grass. In the background, taxis and morning buses rumbled by, cars careened around corners, and in the distance police sirens wailed. Then the most miraculous thing happened. As if anything more miraculous could. The creature—the woman—looked up at him. And she smiled.

More taxis zoomed by. More rumbling buses loaded down with rumbling people. More sirens, more flashing lights, a screaming fire truck or two. But Allan Quinn Fitzpatrick heard none

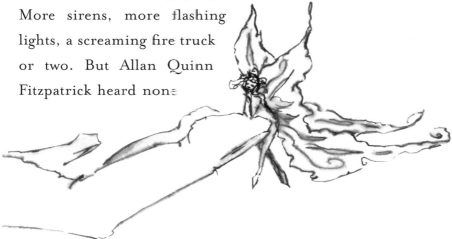

of it. The tiny, tiny woman with golden white wings was smiling at him. And it was as if the sun, for the first time in a century, pierced through a black wall of clouds. He fell back on his heels, spellbound, a childlike grin stretching his face. She was smiling at him, no, *beaming* at him, looking as lovely as anyone possibly could.

2

"...the most important turning points in life
often come in the most unexpected way."
—Napolean Hill

"ALLAN? What's wrong?"

He sat at his desk, mindlessly staring out the window. He'd been this way for hours since fleeing from the park.

"Are you sick? Do you need me to call someone?" Allan looked up into the concerned face of his colleague, a gray-haired man in wire framed glasses. "Say something. Talk to me."

For a split second, he considered blurting out the truth: *Henry, I saw a fairy in Central Park. A damn fairy. Glittering wings and everything!*

"What's going on? Is everything okay at home?"

He grimaced. "Yeah, sure, everything is just fantastic."

His life, of course, was a mess. Sheila had recently

packed her things and moved out; no one wanted to publish his novel; he'd been screwing up royally at his job in the past few months. And now...fairies.

"Maybe you should go." Henry lowered his voice. "The boss hasn't been too happy with you lately."

"What else is new?" Allan shot back. He grabbed his jacket. "Tell him I have the flu." He avoided Central Park on his way home.

That night he decided to treat himself to an early dinner at The Alcove, his favorite downtown bistro in the West Village. The restaurant offered a charming indoor garden decorated with antique oil lamps, scented candles, and intricately designed wrought iron furniture, a pleasant escape from the noise and bustle of the city. He especially appreciated being surrounded by a lush display of baskets and flowerpots overflowing with blooming orchids.

He chose a quiet table in the corner, next to a terracotta planter bursting with exquisite purple and white dendrobiums. He loved those orchids and always made sure to sit near them. Settling in, ordering a glass of red wine, he started feeling more at ease. The horror of the day's events—or rather the day's hallucinations—were beginning to recede. When the waiter delivered his drink Allan barely noticed, never taking his attention from the orchid. He gently touched the blossom's velvety lip.

"It's called a show."

The voice startled him. He looked over to see an elderly woman in her late seventies sitting nearby.

"The orchids," she continued brightly. "When they bloom, it's called a show. Stunning, isn't it? Makes you want to just stand up and applaud."

She giggled and he noticed, not only her youthful voice, but her very odd outfit. First there was the hat. The type leprechauns wear. This was a bit shorter, more stylish, a lustrous green velvet to match the rest of her peculiar clothes. There it sat, complete with a shiny gold buckle, slightly lopsided atop her head. Her hair, silver-gray, was pulled neatly into a bun. She was striking for her age and Allan could easily imagine how attractive she must have been as a younger woman. He took in the rest of her quirky ensemble. A chic brocade and velvet jacket, in distinctive shades of green, with multicolored flowers embroidered across the front. His attention immediately shifted to the wide lapel, an unusual brooch fastened there, round and gold. He couldn't quite make out the design etched within the circle. From where he sat, it looked like an abstract figure, perhaps a dancer, arms raised overhead, with a red stone as the heart. But the figure seemed to have three legs. Trying not to be conspicuous, he leaned slightly forward.

"You like it," the old woman said. It was not a question at all. She rocked toward him, offering a closer look. "Go on," she urged.

He smiled awkwardly, putting on his reading glasses. It wasn't a human figure at all. The design appeared to be a detailed engraving of a tree. What he thought were two arms and a head were actually three branches extending from the trunk. And what looked like legs were three exposed roots. The tree itself was silver, sterling probably, by its rich sheen, with a few tiny greenish gold leaves adorning the branches. A blood red ruby glittered in the center of the trunk.

Allan nodded. "Very unique."

She affectionately patted the pin. Noticing her green velvet gloves, yellow, pink, and purple flower petals stitched across the wrist, he smiled politely. This woman looked as if she just returned from a costume party. Yet in an odd way she also seemed to blend in with the potted trees and flourishing plants, as if she owned the cafe, as if this were her private garden.

"Are you dining alone?" she asked. He wasn't in the

mood for company, but for some reason he invited her to join him. "I thought you'd never ask," she said, pulling up a heavy wrought iron chair beside him. "It's so delightful to see a handsome man like yourself enjoying the dendrobiums. Not everyone appreciates them like you do."

He winked, turning on the charm. "Then they'd have to be blind."

"Oh, no, not blind," she replied. "Simply not present." She noticed the perplexed look on his face. "Enjoying those orchids, you were present. You were in your heart."

It was with *heart* he realized she had a slight accent. English or Irish. He wasn't sure. He nodded, though he had no idea what she meant.

"You pretend you understand," she said, "but you don't." Her eyes twinkled. "And you're pretending that as well."

He was thoroughly confused. "I'm sorry but I really—"

"No worries," she said, laughing. "You will soon enough. That's why you're here."

When the waiter came by to take their order, he already regretted having dinner with this eccentric woman.

"I'll have the filet mignon."

"Oh, no," she insisted. "No meat for you tonight. Let me order for both of us." She winked at the waiter. "Two vegetarian house specials, Frederick. For myself and Mr. Fitzpatrick."

He stiffened. "How do you know my name? I didn't—"

"I know lots of things," she replied mysteriously.

"Really?" he said, deciding to humor her. "And what else do you know?"

"I know," she began, "that you're unhappy. Things in your life have not exactly worked out as planned."

He chuckled, uncomfortable. "Well, no one's life is perfect."

She ignored his remark. "Something is missing in your life, isn't it?" She moved closer. "Something you've been yearning for but can't quite find. A secret. A secret you'd be willing to die for."

A flush of heat crept over him. Had someone turned up the temperature? What the hell was she talking about?

"Allow me to introduce myself." Reaching into a beaded purse, she pulled out a silver business card and handed it to him. In the soft candlelight, the card seemed to glow. He slipped his reading glasses back on. Four words floated in the center of the silvery background. Four words stamped in dark green ink: ETHEL GOODWOMAN, FAERIE SPECIALIST.

He leapt to his feet, flinging the card as if it had burst into flames, jarring the table, knocking over a glass of water.

"Good lord, man!" Mrs. Goodwoman exclaimed, dabbing the stream before it spilled onto her lap. "I didn't think it would startle you that much." She touched his arm. "Sit down, Allan. I'm not going to bite you."

He didn't remember sitting. He couldn't seem to remember anything. Like how he arrived at the restaurant. Had he grabbed a cab? Taken the bus? "How could you possibly...where did you...?"

The waiter arrived with napkins and fresh water. "Thank you, Frederick," Mrs. Goodwoman said, then turned her full attention to Allan. "How I know your name is not important. What's important is that you've been chosen."

"Chosen? For what? The psychiatric ward?" He tried to stand again but she pressed her hand on his.

"My, my, you are a scattered fellow, aren't you? How on earth do you expect to survive the Quest if you can't sit still in a cafe?"

"Survive the..." He peered, in disbelief, at this weird old woman. I'm dreaming, he assured himself, dreaming of Tinkerbells in Manhattan and senior citizens in leprechaun hats. He took a deep breath. I'm not going crazy. I'm not having a nervous breakdown. Been drinking too much, that's all. I'll wake up soon, in my own messy apartment, where everything is normal. He willed himself to concentrate. Voices of diners talking, muted laughter, forks and spoons scraping dishes, his chest pounding. I'll be okay. This isn't really happening. I'm just imagining it. He looked across the table. She was still there, awash in green velvet, smiling broadly. "Oh, God," he groaned. "What have I done to deserve this?"

3

"Resistance 's the first step to change."
—Louise Hay

He tossed and turned all night, the day's events spinning in his head like a whirling dervish. First, a disturbing butterfly woman in the middle of Manhattan. Then a kale and beet salad with a gray-haired lunatic making bizarre proclamations about a quest. He glanced at the clock beside his bed. 3:17 am. No way he'd get a wink of sleep. Gripped with an urge to make some tea, he headed to the kitchen. He didn't really like tea, but Sheila had left a few boxes behind. Somehow the idea seemed comforting. He filled the ceramic tea kettle, hers as well, turned on the burner, and began to pace. Whenever he was upset, the motion seemed to relax him. Striding back and forth past the sink and counter, he stayed in the kitchen for a while, then walked into the bedroom. This is ridiculous, he thought. Tomorrow I'm going to a shrink. A few prescription pills and all this will go away.

The tweed sports coat he'd worn to dinner lay draped across a chair. He remembered the silver business card. "What was her name again?" Everything after the spilled water became a blur. Why did he have this vague feeling she stuck something in his jacket pocket? All he could recall was tossing a few twenty-dollar bills onto the table and dashing out of the cafe. He looked at the brown weave of the coat's pocket, his jaw tightening. Maybe it was just a terrible nightmare. Maybe this elderly woman didn't actually exist. If he had conjured up Tinkerbell, why couldn't he fabricate an old lady in a leprechaun hat? Hesitantly, he moved closer to the chair, then slipped his hand inside the pocket. Empty! It was a hallucination. The thought both scared and relieved him. He'd just have to check into a rehab for a few days. People do that all the time. He'd already eased up on the heavy drinking. Tossed out the extra bottles. Maybe things would turn out okay.

He reached into the other pocket. "What the...?" Shocked, he pulled out a white envelope with a silver business card attached by a green paper clip. *Ethel Good-*

woman, *Faerie Specialist.* No phone number, no address. Just four words in a fancy cursive font, stamped in dark green ink. Exhausted, he plopped down on the edge of the bed. The tea kettle whistled. What about the envelope? Had she slid it into his pocket without him knowing? Had he been so freaked out that some nut could actually put her hand in his jacket? Was she some sort of con artist? He turned the envelope over and over, feeling the weight, then held it up to the lamp, trying to see inside. "This is ridiculous." He tore open the flap. The tea kettle begged for attention. Ignoring it, he pulled out...a plane ticket? Dublin Airport? Bewildered, he stared at the thin, stiff paper, then tossed it aside and strode into the kitchen. Rummaging through cabinets, he found a box of tea and turned off the kettle. Why would she give him a ticket to Ireland? Was this some kind of Saint Paddy's Day prank?

He left the mug steaming on the counter and went back to the bedroom.

United Airlines flight 1717. One way. Departing 3/19 at 7:17 PM. "Three nineteen?" Rushing into the kitchen, he grabbed the Kittens & Puppies Calendar that Sheila gave him for Christmas. In a drunken stupor one night he regretfully confessed a fondness for baby animals.

"That's tomorrow!" He pitched the calendar onto the counter. It slid across the surface, colliding with the cup of tea, knocking it to the floor. The mug broke into a dozen pieces. Annoyed, ignoring the mess, he trudged to the bedroom, grabbed the ticket, then hurled it across the room. Like a poorly designed paper airplane, it struck the closet door. Climbing into bed, he switched off the lamp and defiantly pulled the covers over his head. Ireland? Why the hell would he want to go to Ireland?

4

"Destiny is not a matter of chance. It is a matter of choice."
—William Jennings Bryan

THE INTERCOM BUZZED. "Allan, please come into my office."

It wasn't the request itself. Or even the tone of voice. It was the word *please*. Nichols never said please. A gruff, pushy man who had made his way to the top without any apologies to anyone, please was simply not in his vocabulary. Allan knew something was wrong.

"Come in, Allan."

He carefully closed the heavy wooden door behind him and sat down to face a stern-looking, balding man in his sixties.

"How are you, Allan?"

"Fine." He coughed to clear his throat.

"How's Charlotte?"

"Sheila, Mr. Nichols. Her name is Sheila. We broke up."

The older man frowned. "Too bad," he said. "Seemed to be a nice girl."

"You never met her." He was surprised at his own boldness but knew what was coming. "With all due respect, Mr. Nichols, you didn't call me in here to ask about my latest romance."

Nichols sat back in his own custom-made, high-backed, black leather chair. Behind him spanned a wall of glass overlooking the treetops of Central Park. The sunlight streaming into the office made the man looked less imposing. In fact, Allan noticed, he looked weary.

"I'll get right to the point," Nichols said. "We can't afford to keep you any longer. I'm sorry."

Allan clenched his teeth against a sharp wave of emotion. Ten years working for this company and just a simple apology? Nichols slid an envelope across the desk. "Six months' severance pay, Allan. It's generous."

Staring grimly at the envelope, he weighed his options. Tear the check to shreds. Tell Nichols to go to hell. Storm out. But he needed the money. He grabbed the envelope and without looking back, said, "Yeah. Thanks. Have a great life." He marched out, didn't empty his desk, didn't say goodbye to any of his colleagues he'd worked with for so many years.

He headed to Central Park. Almost noon, it bustled

with activity. Young women and teenagers whizzing by on roller blades, skateboards, and bicycles, enjoying the unusually warm day, families picnicking with children, men and women in business attire off on an early lunch break.

Taking slow strides, Allan walked for a long time, turning everything over in his mind. Frankly, he never liked the job. Initially, he accepted the position only until his first novel sold, until the big advance rolled in. But the years piled up, like discarded manuscripts. He began convincing himself he enjoyed the work, the steady salary, and that he was pretty damn good at it—at least until the last seven months when he began showing up late, missing important meetings. He couldn't blame the drinking. Just like the crazy old woman guessed, he wasn't happy—with anything. Not the job. Not the women. Not with his whole damn life. His boss started sending other people on travel assignments, leaving him to mundane desk work.

Coming out of his whirlwind thoughts, he found himself by the lake, its smooth surface rippling from a family of mallard ducks swimming by. He sat down on an empty bench beneath a tall hawthorn tree, its red berries brightening the bare branches. A pair of speckled starlings nibbled on the winter fruit. Maybe getting fired wasn't such a bad thing. Maybe it was an unexpected stroke of luck.

"Sweetheart," a young mother hollered, hurrying

past the row of benches where he was seated. "Don't go too close to the water!" A curly haired little boy in a red jacket knelt at the edge of the lake.

"Mama," he squealed, pointing to the ducks busying themselves in the middle of the lake, "Look!" The young mother crouched down beside her son as they both watched, fascinated.

Allan observed the scene, triggering a long-forgotten memory. He's five years old sitting on the ground in his backyard staring at a naked patch of soil. It's spring. In one corner of the yard, a giant apple tree shelters a new swing set. Nearby, an old barbecue grill. His mother sits beside him wearing a faded blue apron covered in yellow sunflowers.

"It won't grow," Allan whimpers.

His mother wraps her arm around his small, hunched shoulders. "You have to be patient, sweetheart," she says. "It takes time."

These words mean nothing to him. All he knows is that his kindergarten teacher promised he could grow a peapod. She told the class how to do it and he had followed her instructions exactly: Take five or six peas from a peapod, lay them on a moist piece of cotton on the windowsill, and after a few days, tiny white feet will sprout. Then plant the sprouted peas in the soil and very soon you'll have your own peapod.

When his mother picked him up that day from school,

they immediately drove to the supermarket where they purchased a pound of fresh peapods. They went home, sat outside on the back porch, and peeled open the pods, eating some peas while tossing others in a large glass bowl. When they were done Allan carefully chose seven peas, wrapping each in moist cotton, just like his teacher said. Three days later, much to his astonishment, tiny white feet sprouted. Thrilled, he ran outside and planted them in his little makeshift garden. Then, in the spirit of all eager young children, he sat on the ground and waited. After a few hours, he grew tired. The next day, after school, he waited again. Day after day, he did the same thing, at first so excited he could barely keep still. But as the days passed and the soil remained bare, a terrible disappointment began to build.

One afternoon, his mother took him by the hand and led him into the backyard. They knelt by the empty patch of soil. His father sat on an old wooden rocking chair on the back porch, reading the newspaper. "I have an idea," his mother said. Allan wouldn't even look at her. "I think you need to talk to the peapod fairy."

He lifted his sad face. "Why?"

"Because she lives inside the peapod."

"She does?" He squinted at the bare spot.

"Of course, she does," his mother said jubilantly. "All the plants and trees and flowers have fairies living inside them. That's how they grow."

Allan's father, a burly man with thick eyebrows and huge hands, looked up and frowned. "Stop filling the child with foolishness, Becky."

"It's not foolishness!" she shot back.

Allan touched the moist earth. "What do I tell her?" he asked, trying to imagine a tiny, winged creature hidden beneath the dirt.

"Just thank her for taking care of your peapod. And ask her to help it grow strong."

Allan's father shoved the newspaper aside and stood up in a huff. Grabbing his son's hand, he marched him into the living room where a dusty set of Encyclopedia Britannica took up an entire bookshelf. Allan listened to detailed explanations of photosynthesis and cell division, examining confusing diagrams with too many words. Though he couldn't understand anything, he loved sitting beside his father on the couch, listening to his deep, resonant voice.

Later that night, Allan climbed out of bed and snuck into the backyard. Kneeling close to the barren garden, he whispered, "Please peapod fairy, make my peapod grow."

Over the next few days, the soil remained bare. By the time the family left to visit Allan's grandparents in Manhattan for spring vacation, Allan had given up. Though their time in the city was spent visiting museums, taking evening strolls, and eating in wonderful restaurants, all he could think about was how his teacher and mother made promises they could not keep.

After returning home on a Sunday afternoon, he wouldn't even venture into the backyard. Only the enticing smell of grilled burgers finally brought him outside. Halfheartedly, with hands in his pockets and head bowed, he wandered over to the little garden. When he started screaming at the top of his lungs, his mother thought for sure he'd been stung by a bee.

"Mama! Mama!" he cried, over and over. In her rush to see what happened, she knocked a plate of hamburger patties onto the ground. "Mama! Look!" When she reached him, he was sprawled on his stomach in the dirt, eyes wide as saucers. A small green plant, six inches tall, poked out of the soil. "A peapod!" he sang. "A peapod!" They sat beside the newborn plant and gently opened one of the three tiny pods that jutted out from the stem. Inside were six tender green pearls. "Peas!" he cried, eyes blazing with wonder. "Real peas!" His mother kissed him on the cheek.

"Sometimes the magic works slowly," she said, "and all you can do is wait patiently and believe."

A police siren jarred

him out of the memory. The curly-haired boy and his mother were gone. A knot of sadness caught in his throat. He hadn't thought about his mother in a long time. She died of leukemia when he was only seven years old. As much as he tried to fight it, the memory of her last days washed over him.

She lay in a hospital bed, her body thin and pale, skin almost translucent. Though he was old enough to comprehend the tragedy, he was too young to accept it. "You can't die," he sobbed, curled up next to her in bed. "I won't let you."

Tenderly stroking his hair, she said softly, "Don't be afraid. I'm going to a beautiful place, a garden, where it's always spring."

Allan never told anyone what he did every night after he came home from the hospital. Once his father went to sleep, he snuck into the backyard. Down on his knees, in the light of the full moon, he prayed to the peapod fairy.

"Please," he begged from the deepest place in his young heart, "make mama well. I'll do anything. Just make her well."

But on a peaceful spring day in late April, when tulips were in bloom and butterflies flickered like dappled snow, his mother passed away. And with it, Allan's faith in the possibility of magic.

A pair of ducks honked loudly, furiously flailing their wings, startling him back to the present. He watched them for a long time, feeling numb and unsettled by the memory, as they splashed and flapped noisily in the water. His attention wandered to the grass by his feet where he noticed a cluster of tiny four-leaf clovers. Funny, he thought, in all his years of traveling overseas, he had never been to Ireland.

"Then maybe you ought to go."

He twisted around to see who was there. No one.

"Must have imagined it," he muttered.

"Don't you wish."

This time he jumped up, hands raised, as if being held at gunpoint. "Who said that?" Head whipping left and right. "Who's there?"

"It's me, Allan. Up here."

He glanced at the hawthorn tree. Perched comfortably on a low hanging naked branch...

"Oh my God!" Stumbling backwards, he collapsed onto the bench.

The diminutive woman smiled. "You don't seem pleased," she said.

He vigorously shook his head, as if to dislodge what he was seeing.

Then that sweet, lilting voice. "Stop fighting it, Allan."

Slowly, very slowly, he looked up again. And there she was. The itsy-bitsy woman with delicate filigree wings. No, he pleaded silently I can't be seeing this.

She stood up, raising to her full two-inch height, dusted herself off, and pointed one of her dainty little feet. With the grace of a ballerina, tipped slightly forward, she lifted off the branch like a stunning, exotic butterfly. Allan watched helplessly as she fluttered closer to him.

He could do nothing except stare, incredulously, unable to comprehend what he was seeing—a breathtaking miniscule woman, with adorable dimples (which appeared only when she smiled), sapphire blue eyes, and long pale hair, the color of moonlight. Everything about her seemed perfectly formed, even the shape of—Allan stopped in mid-thought, frightened he had gone completely insane.

"Don't worry," she said in a matter-of-fact tone. "You're not insane. The world you're living in is. But believe me, Allan, you're not."

The intelligence of her response—and the fact that she seemed to be reading his mind—both mesmerized and horrified him. He continued to stare. "I look this way," she offered, "because this is how your mind expects me to look." Then she fluttered so close to him, his eyes crossed, and he could feel the breeze from her wings tickling the tip of his nose. Still, he couldn't speak.

"For the love of trees, Allan, snap out of it!" She clapped her hands twice. On the second clap, he coughed as if someone slapped him hard on the back. "Much better," she piped. Satisfied, she settled comfortably

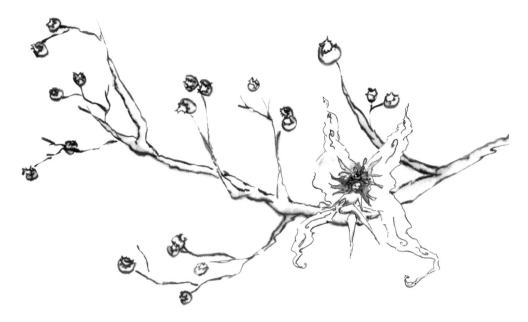

right beside him on the top of the bench. "Now, let's get started." With a wisp of authority, she declared, "We've got a lot of meadow to cover."

Something about her tone reminded him of the crazy lady from the restaurant. He tried to push that out of his mind. Clearly, he was having a serious hallucination. He looked up. Blue sky. Puffy cumulous clouds. A flock of white birds soaring overhead. Everything perfectly ordinary. Nervously, he glanced sideways to see if the creature was still there. Much to his dismay, she was. How could it be, he pondered, that everything looked so normal, yet he was sitting in Central Park beside a miniature woman with wings?

Making sure he was completely alone, he decided, although he had no idea why, to ask the creature a question. As the words tumbled out of his mouth, he

immediately regretted speaking aloud, panicked someone would see him talking to no one and call the police.

"Do you...do you have a name?"

"A name?" Her dot-sized forehead crinkled in thought. "Why, no. We have no need of names."

He wondered what she meant by *we*. Perhaps if there was one of her, there may be more of her. A whole nation, for all he knew. A nation of nameless, thumb-sized, dimple-cheeked women with glittering butterfly wings. When he realized he was giving serious attention to this utter insanity, a wave of intense fear crashed over him.

Being a fairy, she could, of course, hear his thoughts. It wasn't that she was eavesdropping. Fairies would never be that nosy. It was just that she was made up of the same stuff his thoughts were and so they wiggled right past her, making themselves known.

"If it makes things easier for you," she said kindly, "you can call me Faery."

"Okay, then." Still in a state of shock, he mouthed, "Fairy."

"That's Faery with an e," she emphasized. "F-a-E-r-y. If you're going to call me by a name, Allan, please spell it properly."

Her remark plunged him over the edge. Now the

delusion was spell checking him?! An onslaught of nonsensical images followed: Interviews on the 6'oclock news. Tell us, Mr. Fitzpatrick, how often do you chat with Tinkerbell? His Upper West Side neighbors picketing outside his building, waving angry hand-painted signs: Allan Quinn Fitzpatrick is clinically insane! What's next? Aliens on Wall Street?

"Look, Allan," she began in a gentle tone, "I know this must be difficult for you. But we don't have much time. You still have to go home and pack."

Exasperated, he glanced up, talking more to himself than to her. "For what? The space shuttle?"

"Don't be silly. You've got a plane to catch tomorrow."

Was he actually having this bizarre conversation? He looked around again. People doing all sorts of regular sane things—walking dogs, pushing strollers, playing frisbee. "Oh, right, yeah, a plane. That mysterious ticket. Ireland or bust."

She beamed. "Precisely!"

Even if he was, in fact, in the middle of some grave mental breakdown, he couldn't ignore his escalating curiosity. "And for what reason am I flying off to the emerald isle? To rescue a damsel, perhaps, from a fire breathing dragon?"

"Of course not," she replied. "You must go to Ireland for much more serious reasons."

For a split second, he allowed himself the luxury of contemplating what she said. "More serious reasons. I see." He glanced across the lake, at the gleaming Manhattan skyline. "Like what for instance? To save the world?" He chuckled, waiting for some inane reply.

"Exactly." That was all she said.

"Excuse me?"

She spun around, wings vibrating with an air of nonchalance. "You're excused," she replied cheerfully. Floating ahead of him, she added, "Come along, Allan. We don't have much—"

"Wait a second!"

Her wings ceased fluttering and she just hung in midair, a feat not uncomplicated for even a fairy. "Yes?"

He knew this was getting seriously out of hand, but he couldn't help himself. He checked again to make sure no one was nearby.

"Can we take that again, please? Did you say exactly?'"

"Yes. Exactly."

"Exactly like in, yes, exactly, Allan, you have to go to Ireland to save the world?"

She nodded. "Yes. Exactly." He glared at her, irritation and disbelief mounting. What the hell was he doing? Who did he think he was really talking to? Save the world? He desperately needed to get a grip on reality. "What's wrong, Allan?"

"What's wrong!?" he bellowed, the air from his voice

pushing her higher like a miniature kite. "What's wrong is that I'm having a wacko conversation with an aberration named Fairy!" He stomped away.

She flapped furiously to keep up with him. "First of all, Allan, as I already told you, it's Faery with an e, not an i. Secondly— "

"You're actually correcting my spelling again?"

"Yes."

"Wow, my delusions are something else."

"I am not a delusion!" she insisted. "And you need to understand—"

"I don't need to understand anything! If you think I'm getting on a plane because some insect mirage and what's-her-name in a Halloween costume wants me to save the planet, you're even crazier than I am!"

"But Allan!" she cried. "You've been chosen!"

"Horseshit!" He quickened his pace.

"Please don't use that expression," she said, catching up to him. "Horse manure is not a curse, you know. It makes the most beautiful gardens grow."

"Fantastic!" he blurted, taking off in a jog. "Now I've got an environmentally conscious delusion!"

Stay calm, he repeated silently. Focus on rational thoughts. Pharmaceuticals can help. You'll find yourself a top-notch psychiatrist. After a few weeks, you'll be good as new.

"Allan!" When he looked up, she was hovering at eye

level, wings beating like a hummingbird. "Where are you going?"

"None of your damn business." Jogging faster, he kept his attention on the ground slipping under his feet. "Just a delusion," he said over and over. "Don't answer back."

"You can't run away," she pleaded. "We need you!"

He burst into a sprint, running as fast as he could, as if he were being chased by killers, running faster and faster until he was sweating profusely, running through the park, dodging joggers and kids, running out of the park, cutting off taxis and bicyclists, running down his block and dashing up the stairs to his brownstone. Panting heavily, he didn't stop, locking the door behind him, fastening all the bolts. Frantically he shut the windows, pulling down the shades. When he was certain his apartment was secure, he began rummaging wildly through bureau drawers and closets looking for a bottle of anything to drink. In his recent decision to ease up, he had tossed out everything. "Got to have one somewhere," he whined, ripping through kitchen cabinets and under sinks. He found half a bottle of bourbon hidden in the back of the hallway closet. Grabbing a dirty glass from the pile of week-old dishes in the sink, he hurried to the living room. "I'm gonna enjoy this." He flung himself down on the couch, tossed off his shoes, tore off his tie and jacket and poured himself a glass. As he brought the liquid to his lips, his hand began shaking. He tried to lift the glass, but something prevented him. Gritting his teeth, he tried to ignore it. He couldn't, as if someone were right there, in the room, looking over his shoulder.

"Leave me alone!" he shouted. He just wanted a drink. Why couldn't he have one drink? "Damn!" In a fury, he hurled the glass across the room. It shattered against the brick fireplace. What was happening? For God's sake, what was happening?

He knew the answer before he'd even finished the question. What if all this is not a hallucination? What if he's not losing his mind? What if something extraordinary is happening? What if a chance—a chance of a lifetime—is being offered? Was he going to drink it away because he was too scared?

Out of nowhere, ethereal harp music startled him. Nervously, he glanced around the room as if some apparition might suddenly materialize. He forgot it was Sheila's annoying ringtone. She'd chosen it. Irritated, he answered. "What do you want?"

The woman's voice at the other end hesitated. "Allan? It's me. Sheila."

"Yeah, no kidding." He walked into the kitchen to make some coffee.

"Don't get so excited. You might have a coronary."

"I wish."

"Look, Allan, let's be adults about this. I just need to stop by. I left some photo albums in the closet and a few other things." His body stiffened. She was the last person he wanted to see. One look at him and the apartment, she'd know something was terribly wrong.

"No."

"No? What do you mean, no?"

He eyed the broken mug on the floor from last night. The tea bag lay beside it in a puddle. Attached to the tea bag was a short white string with a square paper tag at the end of it. In bold white letters the tag read: IRISH BREAKFAST TEA.

"Allan, what's going on?"

Staring at the tag, his adrenaline pumping, a slight smile tugged at his lips. "I mean, no, Sheila, I won't be here when you come. I'm leaving."

"Leaving? For where?"

He bent down and picked up the soggy tea bag by the paper tag. He held it in front of his face, letting it swing back and forth like a pendulum.

"Where are you going?" He didn't respond. "Allan, answer me. Where are you going?"

"Ireland."

He ended the call, never looking away from the tea bag, watching it swing back and forth with the stable rhythm of a metronome, back and forth, like the brass weight of a grandfather clock, back and forth, as if trying to hypnotize himself, back and forth. "Am I really going to Ireland?"

Somewhere in the deepest, most hidden part of him, a faint voice answered Light, sweet. Almost musical.

Yes. Yes. Yes.

5

"A hero is someone who has given his or her life
to something bigger than oneself."
—Joseph Campbell

THE INTERNATIONAL TERMINAL at Kennedy airport resembled a Woodstock reunion. Hordes of young people in tie-dyed T-shirts and colorful sweatpants sprawled out on the carpeted floor, well-worn backpacks beneath their heads, eager to board their planes. Throngs of tired families carrying pillows and whining children, waiting, forever it seemed, to go home.

Allan sat at the bar, sipping a draft beer, trying to convince himself he was doing the right thing. Yesterday when Sheila called, the idea of flying to Ireland didn't seem like an outlandish decision. But being in the airport, watching everyone rushing around, doubt and uncertainty were starting to take hold. When he first arrived, he hesitated to check in, approaching the counter at least half a dozen times and walking away. When he handed over the ticket—who the hell uses paper tickets anyway—he finally relaxed. The bubbly brunette confirmed the reservation: window seat with a preselected vegetarian meal.

Nibbling mindlessly on peanuts at the bar, he went over everything again. Why not go? He could use a change of scenery, a new perspective. At the very least, it would be an adventure—he couldn't wrap his head around the notion of a quest. He was strong, fit, intelligent, more than capable of figuring out most things, why couldn't he do this? Besides, traveling around Ireland might just be the very thing he needed to recharge, boost his spirits, maybe even motivate him to dive back into writing.

"Another beer, sir?"

"No, thanks." He needed to be as calm and clear-headed as possible. He still wasn't absolutely convinced that the winged creature and old woman were one hundred percent real. He decided that even if this was some creepy delusional episode, what did he really have to lose? He already lost his job and girlfriend. He needed a break.

As he pulled out his wallet to pay the check, he thought he saw a woman in a green hat disappear into the restroom. Sliding a twenty-dollar bill under his glass, he hurried over to the entrance. Could that be her? Ethel what's her name? He had shredded her business card the other night thinking it could be evidence of his lunacy. The woman never came back out. When he heard the second boarding call for flight 1717, he headed to the gate.

A long line of passengers snaked through the waiting area—couples, infants, teenagers, grandparents, everyone chatting excitedly. The crowd annoyed him. As he stepped into the jetway, something prompted him to turn around. There she was, over by the restrooms, waving a green handkerchief. "See you soon, dearie!" Ethel Goodwoman called out.

"Wait!" he shouted. But the stream of people trapped him like a leaf in a strong current. Once aboard the plane he took his seat, glad that no one was sitting beside him yet. As people ambled by, dragging luggage, he felt a growing anxiety. Would she show up? Hadn't she said, see you soon? Why would she be at the airport if she wasn't joining him? Had he imagined everything? When the last of the stragglers boarded, and the adjacent seat remained empty, he let out a sigh of relief. It would be a seven-hour flight and he was in no mood to make pointless conversation. He began rummaging through the seat pocket, hoping to find something distracting to read. Nothing except a safety brochure and crumpled cocktail napkin. About to shove the napkin back into the seat pocket, he noticed some writing, neat and large, in black marker: Accept uncertainty and life will be good.

When the flight attendant stopped by to see if he needed anything, he absent-mindedly stuffed the napkin into his jacket and asked for a cup of coffee.

Takeoff was uneventful. He didn't really like flying. Being confined for so many hours drove him a little crazy. Settling into the flight, he found himself imagining what Ireland would be like: verdant rolling hills, quaint pubs, and hopefully, a pretty Irish lass or two. But no matter how involved he became in his thoughts, he invariably found himself drifting back to...*chosen*...and that conversation in the park. Hadn't the Ethel woman said the exact same thing?

Dinner was an unappealing tray of lukewarm vegetables over tofu. He hardly noticed the meal because he couldn't stop watching an elderly couple sitting across the aisle. Well-dressed, and probably in their eighties, they looked like seasoned travelers, so comfortable with each other, sharing their food and talking softly. Watching them, he thought of his mother. She would have been happy knowing he was going to Ireland. As a little boy, he often snuck into the living room during her afternoon nap. She was the most beautiful woman in the world to him. He loved her silky red hair and striking green eyes. Irish to the bone, she used to say. At night, tucking him into bed, she'd often tell him stories about the old country, promising one day they'd visit. He remembered the sadness in her voice, as if she knew it would never be.

Allan watched as the elderly woman lay her head gently on her husband's shoulder. When the old man coughed, shifting in his seat, and forcing her to reposition, Allan began thinking about his father.

After his mother passed, the two of them lived together in a small apartment, fighting all the time. Dozens of times, Allan tried to run away, wondering desperately why it hadn't been his father who died that day.

Born to a poor Polish Jewish family, his father immigrated to the United States as a child. Allan never could understand why his mother married him. A few weeks after her death, everything started to change drastically. His father began selling and donating all of her favorite dishes because he wanted to keep a kosher kitchen. He started attending synagogue every Friday and Saturday, demanding Allan go as well. It wasn't the religious changes that disturbed Allan so profoundly.

As a small boy he loved the Jewish holidays as much as the Christian ones. Instead, it was the terrible fact that his father wanted to extinguish, wipe away, eradicate anything that had to do with his mother. He sold the house Allan grew up in, got rid of all her cherished linens and crystal, and Allan was never again permitted to mention anything even remotely Irish.

For decades Allan carried a photograph of his mother that he took as a little boy one afternoon when they had visited Central Park together. She was standing under a blossoming cherry tree, the lake sparkling in the background, her head back, laughing. She looked like an angel. He kept the photo in his wallet for years. Occasionally a jealous girlfriend would discover it, certain that the beautiful woman was a favored ex-lover. In his twenties and thirties, he brought the faded photograph into session after session with therapists, talking bitterly about his father and describing all the reasons why they could never get along.

Whenever a therapist tried to delve deeper, asking him to talk about the day his mother died, he shrugged it off or spit out excuses: can't remember, too many decades ago. Every psychologist clearly saw what he couldn't; her death had burned him, like a wildfire, leaving only a blackened veil shrouding his heart.

If they brought up his father, suggesting he might

have some anger issues, it always ended the same way. He'd storm out of the room, slamming the door behind him. Allan smirked at the memory. Of course, he had issues. Who wouldn't with a father like that? An insensitive, overbearing man, heartless, who treated him like a child when he was a grown man, but never treated him like a child when he needed it most. It was his father who clearly needed therapy, not him.

Even in the last days of his father's life, the tension between the two of them never eased. The mere mention of his mother would send them into a shouting match. Allan hated his father for that, hated his stubborn, righteous ways. Hated him so much that the day after he died, Allan went straight to the county court to legally change his name to his mother's maiden name. Fitzpatrick. That wasn't enough, though. His mother had given him a middle name which his father despised. "You're a Quinn," she announced the day he was born. "It means wisdom. You're a wise old soul." Growing up, his father never permitted him to use Quinn. So, the morning Allan buried his father was the morning Allan Quinn Fitzpatrick was born.

"More coffee?" the flight attendant asked. It took him a moment to pull himself back to the present.

"No. Thank you."

He needed to stretch, move his body. He detested thinking about the past. As far as he was concerned, therapy and personal growth were a waste of time and money. What's the point, he thought, walking to the back of the plane. You can't change things. What's done is done.

A group of men were chatting in front of the bathrooms. In no mood to interact, he stepped inside a vacant lavatory and locked the door. He glanced briefly in the mirror, then splashed cold water on his face, imagining, with amusement, Sheila's reaction to the apartment. The broken mug and shattered glass were still on the floor. As he reached for a paper towel, he shrieked. Because there she was, looking as dainty as ever.

A flight attendant immediately knocked on the door.

"Sir, everything all right in there?"

Allan stammered, "Yeah, fine. I'm...fine." Lowering his voice, he said, "How the hell did you get in here? We're 35,000 feet in the air!"

Faery puffed out her chest. "We do have certain abilities," she said proudly. "Anyway, you ran off quickly in the park and there's so much more I must tell you. First of all, when you arrive in Dublin—"

He held up his hand to stop her. They were in an airplane bathroom, for God's sake! The madness of the situation intensely disturbed him. Maybe getting on the plane wasn't such a good idea after all.

"It was a very good idea," she insisted. "Now, once in Dublin, we want you to—"

"I'm a grown man. I don't need directions."

"Oh, but you do. You need our help with—"

"With what? Saving the planet?"

"Oh, no," she said, shaking her head. "We couldn't help you with that. Completing the Quest is up to you. No one can help you with that. We can only give you advice." Carefully, she climbed onto the stainless steel counter.

Turning on the faucet, he began vigorously washing his hands again.

"Look, Faery with an e. The only reason I decided to do this was because I needed a vacation. That's all. Maybe a week or two, take in a few sights, visit a few castles, buy a couple of woolen sweaters…" His voice trailed off.

"Now, Allan," she said, sounding a bit schoolmarm-ish, "you know as well as I do that that's not why you're here."

He snatched out towel after towel. Why was it that everything she said irritated him?

"Once you arrive in Dublin," she continued with great patience, "there won't be any time for shopping. You've got a mission to focus on."

"Right, a mission,' he grumbled loudly. "So who am I now? James frickin' Bond?!"

Startled, Faery stepped backwards, bumping into the mirror. "Allan," she stuttered. "I don't know anyone called James frickin Bond."

Something infinitesimal glistened on her cheek. "I'm sorry," he said, bending down. "I didn't mean to be…it's just that…"

Her face brightened. (Fairies never hold grudges). "Thank you."

Just then, someone pounded on the door. "Hey, mister!" demanded a gruff male voice. "There's other people waitin' out here! You done yet?"

"No!" Allan shouted. "I got unfinished business!" He double-checked the lock. "Look, Faery…" He sighed, shaking his head in bewilderment. "There's a part of me that still thinks this is all one huge horrifying delusion. That I've gone off the deep end. That any second, I'm gonna wake up, drooling, in a padded cell." He tried to pace. There wasn't any room, so he dropped the toilet seat and sat down. "Then there's another part of me, a really small part, mind you, I mean really small, even smaller than you, that thinks, maybe, just maybe I'm not totally bonkers. Maybe you do exist. Maybe for some unknown reason, a reason I'll never figure out in a million years, a frickin' fairy and green velvet lady want me to go to

Ireland." He laughed and that made her smile. "But," he added in a more somber tone, "if you think I'm going there to fight some evil force or troupe of Darth Vaders out to destroy the planet, you and Ethel Goodfellow have another thing coming!"

"Goodwoman," she said gently.

"Yeah, well, whatever."

Her eyes filled with tears. "It's not like what you're saying at all. You're not going to Ireland to save the earth from...from evil forces or—"

"Then what?" He was losing patience. "What the hell do you want me to save the earth from?"

Hesitating, her face scrunching into the teeniest frown, she burst out crying. "From...from...from being overlooked!"

He frowned, confused. "Overlooked?"

She nodded, wiping her cheeks with the tips of her wings.

"People," she began, stepping closer, wings shivering, "have forgotten us." Her delicate shoulders drooped. "They've just forgotten us."

"Forgotten? What do you mean?"

She walked right up to his face, stopping a hair's breadth from his nose. "The trees, the flowers, the shrubs!" she burst out passionately. "The blades of grass, the leaves, the rivers, the clouds, everything! They've forgotten all of us!"

He searched his mind for some comforting words. "That's not true. People see stuff like that all the time. If you mean nature, well, people haven't forgotten nature. We build parks, go on picnics. It's not at all what—"

"No!" She crossed her arms against her chest in a stance of defiance. "We've been overlooked. All of us. No one sees the Hidden Kingdom anymore. No one really looks at us anymore." Her voice ached with sadness. "No one praises us anymore."

He sighed, even more perplexed. "The hidden what? I don't understand."

"People have become too busy. Too hurried. Too full of anger and despair. Maybe for a few, we're background, a pretty setting to take a nap. But that's not enough!" She paused and her voice became barely audible. "We're dying, Allan. All of us. We're dying from being overlooked."

He stood up, trying to comprehend what she meant. Part of him was convinced she was completely wrong. Take Central Park. People out there all the time, day and night, jogging, biking, taking afternoon strolls. He had lots of friends who liked to go to the country or rent cabins in the woods for weekend getaways.

"That's not good enough!" she cried. "We're dying, Allan. All of us!" She spoke those words with such conviction and such great sadness that it pained him. He thought about all the recent years of terrible news—global warming, decimated rain forests, melting glaciers, toxic rivers, polluted oceans. Sure, things looked bad. But people around the world were doing something about it, weren't they? Kids and teenagers becoming activists, communities and schools building urban gardens. Every few months some new environmental documentary came out on climate change or sustainability, along with piles of best-selling books. Even companies like Walmart have

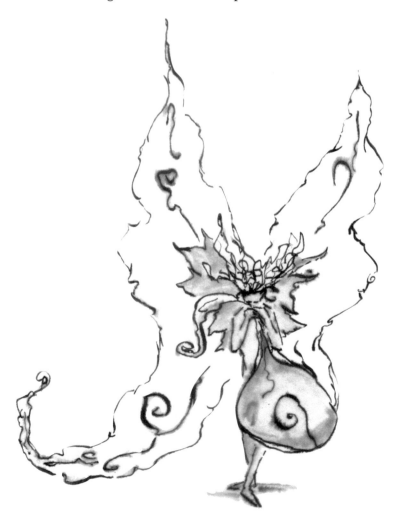

jumped onboard the green movement. And his next-door neighbors were fanatic about composting and recycling, always dragging biodegradable trash bags filled with juice boxes and bottles.

"It's not enough!" Her teeny fingers balled into fists as her cheeks blushed a pale pink. "That's why you have to go, Allan! That's why you have to find the Book! And fill the pages! That's why you have to bring back the Sacred Branches!" She clasped her hands together in a gesture of prayer. "You have to remember what everyone has forgotten."

He didn't know what to say. She was making him more and more upset. What book? What pages? What branches? He had to remember what? The enormity of it overwhelmed him. He needed to be alone, sort things out. "I have to go," he said, fumbling with the lock on the door.

"Allan!"

As the door swung shut, he heard her sad voice trail off. "We need you."

Back in his seat, he pulled down the window shade and tried to cover himself with a ridiculously small blanket. After a nap he'd be able to think more clearly, digest everything that was happening. Quickly, he drifted off to sleep.

He was awakened by the flight attendant. "Sir, we'll

be landing in Dublin soon. Please bring your seatback to an upright position."

Still groggy, he lifted the window shade, looking out at the wide expanse of green below. Ireland. What was in store for him down there?

PART TWO

Initiation

"Once long ago
You sang and danced in the moonlight.
You praised the Truths that grew inside your heart
Like branches on a tree.
You were innocent then.
Remember, please, remember."

—The Ancient Book of Fae

6

"Those who don't believe in magic will never find it."
—Roald Dahl

DUBLIN SKIES WERE GRAY, clouds heavy with rain. Allan stood beneath a concrete overhang, watching the parade of taxi cabs driving down the wrong side of the road. Standing there, suitcase in hand, he realized he had no idea where to go. Tired and feeling a little disheartened, being here didn't seem as exciting as he thought it would.

He reached into his pocket and pulled out the crumpled cocktail napkin: Accept uncertainty and life will be good. Really not a bad piece of advice. He noticed something else written on the back that he must have overlooked. In a much more hurried handwriting, it said O'Sullivan's B&B, 17 Stonecrest Lane. Great stew! Just then, a taxi pulled up. The window rolled down, revealing a chubby cheeked Irishman with a black wool cap. "Mornin' to ya. Would ya' be wantin' a ride?"

Allan looked back down at the napkin. "What the hell." He climbed in. "17 Stonecrest Lane," he said.

"Ah, the O'Sullivans," the driver replied, "a culchie pair, they are."

"Pardon me?"

"A bit of a journey, if you don't mind me saying. Nearly two hundred kilometers south."

Allan frowned. "Oh, well, if that's too far…"

"Don't be worrying about it, it's grand." And they took off.

They drove for hours, past rolling, green fields dotted with cows and horses, past hillside graveyards with Celtic stone crosses and lofty church steeples. As the road narrowed, they passed dozens of crumbling roadside statues of the Virgin Mary blanketed in red and white carnations. Often, they moved at a snail's pace, trapped behind flocks of bleating sheep crossing the road. Soon they were weaving down winding roads bordered by jagged cliffs overlooking a swirling blue-gray ocean. Then more whitewashed cottages appeared and low stone walls that seemed to follow them forever like an endless graying serpent. Even when the rain finally stopped, everything stayed blanketed in a soft haze, making the fields and meadows look almost mystical.

The bed and breakfast was nestled in a wooded glen, and as they pulled up to the old picket fence, the sun broke through the thick wall of clouds overhead. Sunbeams scattered in every direction, illuminating a distant meadow and an expanse of forest just beyond. A stunning backdrop for this thatched roof, stone cottage, with a faded red front door, cobbled walkway, and a brick chimney spewing a thin stream of charcoal smoke.

Edna and Patrick O'Sullivan, a cheerful older couple in their late sixties, welcomed Allan as if he were long lost kin. Mr. O'Sullivan, a lanky man who gave the appearance of being taller than he was, puffed constantly on a pipe while hiding his thumbs beneath a pair of worn black suspenders. The suspenders stretched tightly over too many layers of sweaters in colors that shouldn't match, but somehow did. Mrs. O'Sullivan, the more outgoing of the two, and round in every way, wore a few sweaters as well over a brightly flowered dress with a scarf made of the same material. Both their faces, etched from years of hard work and hard living, still managed to shine with a genuine kindness.

The very first thing they showed Allan was their garden. Though barely spring, every kind of vegetable and flower flourished. It made no sense. It was impossible for anything to be growing this time of year. Frost still glittered on the ground, yet fist-sized roses bloomed on bushes, bright sunflower plants peeked over wire fences, and a stunning display of lilacs and tulips beckoned to all who passed by.

Astounded by the unnatural abundance of beauty, he said, "I'm no gardener but even I know this is not possible. What's your secret?"

Mrs. O'Sullivan laughed, her eyes sparkling. "'Tis magic what makes 'em grow."

"Magic?" he repeated, puzzled.

She beamed. "The magic of music. I sing to 'em every day, from me heart."

Inside the cozy cottage, a large fireplace warmed most of the rooms. Allan noticed an oval plaque above the mantle that was oddly empty, as if it were meant for a trophy fish.

"She was a beauty, she was," Patrick O'Sullivan said, noticing Allan's puzzled look. "But the missus, she carried on, givin' out, beggin' me to let it go." He lit up his pipe again, puffing hard, a sweet, smoky aroma filling the room.

Allan smiled awkwardly. "Nice plaque, though." The Irishman shrugged, then sat down in a large, faded armchair and went back to reading his book.

Mrs. O'Sullivan led him to his room, explaining there were only two extra bedrooms, both upstairs, that she and her husband slept downstairs in a small room off the kitchen, and that no other people were booked to arrive anytime in the near future. That was fine with Allan since he wasn't feeling particularly social and didn't think he'd be spending much time at the cottage anyway. The room, small yet pleasant, had an antique iron bed, oak bureau, and a private bathroom. Mrs. O'Sullivan apologized profusely for the idiosyncrasies of the old sink and claw-foot bathtub, showed him how to open and close the wooden shutters that often stuck, and then quickly hurried out.

Allan plopped down on the springy mattress, pleased with his surroundings. He was glad he had chosen this place. Patrick O'Sullivan even offered him an old farm truck to rent, which he eagerly accepted.

He laid down for a short nap and ended up sleeping for hours. The time change and bizarre events in the past week had utterly exhausted him. When he awoke it was evening, about seven. Starving, he stumbled downstairs, finding Mrs. O'Sullivan on the couch, reading.

"Oh, my, you must be hungry," she said, rising quickly. "I've kept some stew in the oven." She ushered him into the kitchen and served him a simple, hearty meal of lamb and potato stew, home-baked soda bread, and pudding for dessert. Allan was grateful. As she poured tea, Mr. O'Sullivan shuffled in, wearing a tattered old robe.

"Evenin'," he said, nodding in Allan's direction. Then he turned to his wife. "Got any pie?"

She took a large fresh apple pie from the pantry and served him a giant slice. "And you, Mr. Fitzpatrick?" He was stuffed but didn't want to be impolite.

"I'd love some."

"So," Patrick O'Sullivan began, his mouth stuffed with pastry. "Special reason brings ya' to Ireland?"

"Paddy!" his wife snapped. "Don't be so nosy."

"Taint a bit nosy." He gulped. "Curious. That's all."

Allan smiled. "That's all right. Just a little R & R." They both looked at him, confused. "Rest and relaxation. It's an American expression."

"Then you'll be wantin' to take your walks," Mrs. O'Sullivan said, sitting down beside him. "We've got an ancient forest nearby.' She paused, looking right at him, "Some say it's full of the wee folk."

Allan coughed, spitting up a piece of crust.

"Now look at what you done!" Mr. O'Sullivan exclaimed. He slapped Allan hard on the back. "Hush that talk!"

Allan coughed a few more times, then sipped his tea. "I'm fine. Really."

Edna O'Sullivan lowered her voice, a strange look on her face. "Go there in the early mornin'. Just 'fore the sun rises."

"Edna!" Patrick O Sullivan slammed his hand down on the table. "C'mere to me, woman. Leave the poor man alone. Go brew some more tea."

Obediently, she busied herself at the stove. Allan stood up.

"I'm really very tired," he lied. "Thanks for supper. It was delicious."

"Good night," she said, smiling. "Sweet dreams."

7

"Remember the sacredness of things,
running streams and dwellings,
the young within the nest,
the holy flame of fire."
—Pawnee Indian Song

IT TOOK HIM HOURS to fall asleep. He lay in bed, staring at patches of fresh white paint on the ceiling. Something about Edna O'Sullivan bothered him. He felt as if she could see right through him. Just like Ethel Goodwoman.

It was a fitful night of disturbing dreams. A woman on fire, beckoning to him. Running toward her, she vanished into dark woods. Then a child, a young girl, dancing with him in the middle of a forest, singing in a language he didn't understand.

He bolted upright, as if someone shouted his name. The large wooden clock on the bureau said 5:17 and he remembered Mrs. O'Sullivan's cryptic advice: Go in the early morning, just before the sun rises.

Restless, he went to the window. In the moonlight he could see, beyond the meadow, the edge of a forest. He stared into the dark, mind quiet, listening to the peaceful night. A walk seemed appealing.

Bundled in a sweater and jacket, he quietly headed out. Stars glittering overhead, breathing in the clear cold air, he could see the beginnings of dawn streaking across the sky. Strolling leisurely, he crossed the meadow. Even though the rising sun lightened the sky, the forest loomed dark and shadowed in front of him. Why go in, he thought uneasily. No need to explore this early. Why not wait until afternoon? He was about to head back when he heard the familiar morning chorus of birds. A well-worn path lay before him, reaching into the woods, assuring that he certainly wasn't the first to enter. He turned up his collar and continued on. With every step, he began to relax, arms swinging loosely at his side, filling his lungs with intoxicating scents of spruce, pine, and cedar trees, pungent and sweet. The tip of his nose and cheeks red from the chill, he felt more alive than he had in ages.

As he came around a bend on the path, he stopped, surprised by a curious sight ahead. A small fire blazed, burning in a perfect circle, about ten feet in diameter. The flames, pure white, burned only a few inches above the ground. Not a hint of orange or red. Weird, he thought, approaching the circle. No heat emanated from the flames. What type of fire could this possibly be?

A pile of leaves, bark, and twigs in the center drew his attention. There was something very unusual about it.

When he stepped closer, he realized what it was. A book!

Without thinking, he stepped over the flames and walked to the spot where it lay. It was the strangest book he had ever seen. About a foot all around, the cover constructed of thick, rough bark, matted with dry leaves. A thin line of fresh moss grew along the edges. The spine of the book, made of short, twisted branches, appeared to be woven together with pine needles, dripping with clumps of sticky golden sap. He wanted to touch it, lift it, but he was afraid it might crumble in his hands. Then he remembered what Faery said to him on the plane: *That's why you have to go. To find the Book.*

Kneeling, he carefully picked it up. It felt surprisingly heavy. As he gently held the book against his chest, a voice surged inside his head: *We have been waiting for You. You who hold these pages in your hands. The time has come. Do not be afraid. You are the Chosen One.*

Clutching the book, he leapt over the fire in one graceful motion. The moment his feet touched the ground, flames shot up toward the sky, then fell to earth like a dead weight, crackling, sizzling, extinguished.

Stunned, he inched closer. No blackened remains, no charred leaves. Nothing hinting a huge fire just burned

there. Not one burnt twig. Not one piece of ash. The area looked like any other peaceful place in a forest.

A bird shrieked, startling him. He bolted, hugging the book tightly, running at full speed. He didn't slow down until he reached the meadow, then collapsed on the grass, panting. Looking up at the clear morning sky, all he could think about was that by some miracle, he'd found the book. No doubt about it. This was the book Faery told him to find. He knew he could do it. This was the reason Faery and Ethel Goodwoman had chosen him. Lifting himself up on one elbow, he admired his treasure. This was the book that must contain answers, secrets, some sort of powerful life-changing wisdom. He couldn't wait another second. As he carefully lifted the coarse wood cover, his only thought was, this quest stuff isn't so hard after all.

8

"When you change the way you look at things,
the things you look at change."
—Wayne Dyer

"**I**t's blank!"

He sat cross-legged on the grass, the book open on his lap, peering at the pages. Blank, all of them. Blank! He looked at every single one, turning each page slowly and with care. They were made of smooth bark, mostly pale, some grainy and discolored, others covered with thin lines of ants crawling across them. Every single page blank.

Now what? He had come all this way. And for what? An old moss-covered pile of sap and twigs without a single word of wisdom? Was this some kind of twisted faery joke? He jumped up, shouting, "Faery! Where the hell are you?" He looked around in every direction, expecting her to flutter down from the sky. Nothing happened. "This is horseshit!" He had crossed a ring of fire. Jeopardized his own well-being. Put his very life at risk to grab some blank, bug-filled book? What kind of quest is this anyway?

"The best kind there is."

He spun around and there she was, lounging on a bright green leaf, basking golden in the sun.

"What's going on?" Allan demanded, scooping up the book. "You told me to find the book and I did. Look, see for yourself."

He set the book down beside her. She stepped closer, letting her fingers brush against the grainy bark.

"It's...it's beautiful," she cooed. "It's been sung about in all our legends and myths. It's been praised since the beginning of forest time. It's exactly as I pictured it." She tenderly placed her cheek on the scratchy surface. "Oh, I can hardly believe it. The Ancient Book of Fae. This is the Book that contains the three Sacred Branches. This is the Book that holds all our wisdom. You found it, Allan. You found it already."

For a moment he felt proud, like a hunter admiring his prey. Then reality hit. "But it's blank, Faery. Every damn page is blank!"

"Yes," she smiled, still full of reverie. "I know."

"You what?"

"I know."

"You know? What the hell do you know?"

Faery backed up, covering her diminutive ears with her hands. "Please, Allan," she begged, "stop shouting." She gestured to the surrounding meadow, "You're hurting us."

He remembered, regretfully, the incident on the plane. "I'm...sorry. I'm just upset. I need you to explain what's going on."

She shrugged. "There's nothing to explain. You just said so yourself. The pages are blank."

"I know they're blank!" The blast from his words sent

her tumbling backwards off the leaf. He knelt to see if she was okay.

Dusting herself off, she said, "Then what's the problem, Allan?"

Exasperated, he sat down beside her. They sat in silence for a long time. She patiently watched him. "The problem," he began wearily, "is that you told me on the plane to find a book that would save the world. And I did. Here it is. But something must have happened. Rain, sun, too many insects, lousy ink, I don't know. The words are simply not there. The pages are totally blank."

"Yes," she said with a bright smile. "That's because you have to fill them in." He glared at her. "Allan, I've been trying to tell you ever since our conversation in the park but you wouldn't listen."

"Fill them in?"

"Yes, of course. Did you think..." She covered her mouth, giggling. "Did you think that the Quest was simply to find the Book?" He felt like a fool. "I'm sorry, Allan, but the Quest has barely begun."

He fell back on the grass.

She let him lay there for the longest time. When he finally turned to look at her, she took that as permission to continue.

"*You* fill the pages, Allan, by discovering the three Sacred Branches."

He pondered her answer. "Sacred branches? So now I have to hunt down some holy tree and chop it to pieces?"

Her eyes widened in horror. "Oh, no," she said, fervently. "The Sacred Branches are our Truths. The Truths we live by. The Truths that people have forgotten. You have to learn them, Allan. That's how you fill the Book."

"Seems to me," he replied, oozing sarcasm, "that I could learn them way better if they were already written down."

"But what good would that do? Truth only has meaning if it lives inside you. That's why the pages are blank."

What she said, of course, made a kind of sense, in a theoretical sort of way.

Forcing himself to speak calmly, he said, "Tell me, Faery, how do I go about doing that? How do I discover these truths of yours?" He lay there, not really expecting any sort of reasonable response.

"That's the Quest," she answered gleefully. "That's why you're here."

Curling into a fetal position, the staccato melody from *Mission Impossible* crept into his mind. Something told him this was going to be a long, complicated journey.

9

"Mystery is the soul of existence."
—Kedar Joshi

HE DIDN'T KNOW how long he lay in the meadow.
When he finally sat up, still dazed, Faery was gone. He'd
had enough bewildering adventures for one morning.
Heading back to the cottage, he vowed to salvage the day,
ignore the fact he was in a foreign country because a
butterfly woman told him to find a mystical scripture that
would save the planet. He glanced down at the book and
decided to forget everything for a few hours. Do a little
sightseeing, act like a tourist, go have some normal fun.

There was no one at the cottage when he returned. It
was much later than he thought. The clock on the kitchen
stove read 11:17 a.m. A neatly written note lay on the
table beside fresh-baked scones and a ring of car keys.

A pot of tea sat on the stove. He smiled, grateful to the O'Sullivans for their hospitality. If he didn't do anything right, at least he ended up at this place. He poured himself a cup of tea, then read the note. "Dear Mr. Fitzpatrick, Hope you enjoyed the forest. Patrick insists the pickup truck is reliable. Don't forget to drive on the left. Yours truly, Edna O'Sullivan."

After two scones, smothered in strawberry jam and clotted cream, his spirits revived. Climbing into the truck, he planned to drive to the nearest town and get himself a pint or two of the famous Irish stout. He had considered leaving the book in his room, hidden under the bed, but the idea of Edna O'Sullivan discovering it made him anxious. The truck sputtered a bit, then started up. With the book beside him, he drove off.

He found a small pub in a nearby village, a quaint brick building with a wooden sign swinging from a rusted chain. The bar was already crowded. Local folks talking, laughing, clutching glasses of dark beer. Nobody seemed to pay much attention to him, and he liked that. He slid into a booth by a window and peered out at the cobblestone street.

"Can I help you?'

He turned and looked up into the face of the most stunning woman he'd ever seen. Struck speechless, he could only stare.

She gazed down at him, emerald eyes shining, and hair, the color of fire, cascading down her shoulders. She wore a white lace dress that touched the floor, making her seem more like a diaphanous goddess than a waitress.

"What is it that you need?" she asked softly. "Tell me."

All he could manage to say was, "I...I...I don't know."

The room began to spin. He gripped the table, trying to regain some sense of balance. If he had believed in Cupid, in love at first sight, he would have acknowledged, right then and there, the poignant arrow that pierced straight through his heart.

When he looked again, she was gone.

"Hey! Wait! I wanted—" A heavy hand touched his shoulder. He twisted around.

Looking down at him now was a puffy woman in her late fifties with a huge bust bursting from a stained white apron. She grinned, showing off a missing front tooth. "Can I help ya'?" Allan ignored her, looking everywhere else.

"Where did she go?" he asked, distraught.

"Who?"

"The other waitress!"

The woman peered at him suspiciously. "Nobody else here 'cept meself."

"Yes, there is!" he exclaimed, surprised at how upset he felt. "She had red hair! The most incredible red hair I've ever seen."

The entire pub fell silent. Dozens of heads turned toward him.

"That ain't funny," the waitress replied, a nasty ring to her voice.

"I didn't mean to be funny." Allan looked around. "I just want to know where she went."

The pub owner, a giant lumberjack of a man, with a wiry red beard and mustache, crashed his fist down on the bar. "Enough!" he bellowed. "Get out o' me pub!"

Allan had no idea what was happening. "But—"

"GET OUT!"

He stumbled toward the door, taking one last glance around to see if she was there.

"OUT!"

Back on the street, he slumped against a brick wall trying to regain his composure. "What the hell?"

"For an American, you got some bullocks."

He looked over to see a teenage boy with bright purple hair standing beside him. A dozen silver earrings poked through both ears. "One more minute in there," the boy said with a thick Irish brogue, "and they woulda ate the head off a' ya."

"What on earth did I do?"

The boy lit a cigarette. "For sure they thought you was slagging 'em." Allan looked confused. "Makin' fun of somethin' awful."

"Why would they even think that?"

"Catherine," the boy replied, exhaling a long thin line of smoke. "You mentioned Catherine."

"Then she was there! The red-haired woman. Why did everyone act so upset?"

"She's dead."

The color drained from Allan's face. "What?"

"She died a year ago today. Catherine Elizabeth Stewart. The pub owner's only daughter."

Everything started to spin. He slid down to the ground.

"Can you get me some water?" he stammered. The boy nodded and hurried into the pub. How could this be? He had seen her, standing right there, beautiful, beyond beautiful...

The boy quickly returned. "If they'd known it was for you, they'd 'ave smashed it over me head."

After a few minutes, he felt better. "Catherine...how did she die?"

The boy shrugged. "No one really knows. Still a mystery. Went off into the woods one day and never came back."

"Then why do they think she's dead?"

"Been a year. What else could have happened?"

Still a bit shaky, he pulled himself to his feet. "There are dozens of possibilities," he insisted. "She could have run off with someone. Or gone to another country. What makes them think—?"

"The police. They found her scarf in the woods. Decided she musta been murdered, probably by some lunatic Englishman, most likely."

After a long silence, Allan handed the boy the empty glass. "Thanks."

"No big deal." He set the glass down by the door and started to leave, then turned around. "If I was you, I'd leg it to another pub. One about five kilometers to the south. No one will bother you there." He walked off, whistling.

Allan hardly remembered driving to the next town. He couldn't stop thinking about the red-haired woman, seeing her face, hearing her voice. When he pulled up in front of the pub, he desperately needed a drink. Glancing down at the book, he debated about leaving it in the truck but decided to take it inside.

Just like the teenager said, nobody bothered him here. He found a table by a window overlooking a narrow alley. Much to his relief, the waitress, an outgoing young girl who looked the same age as the purple-haired boy, had curly blonde hair. She brought him a glass of stout. Still feeling dazed, he sipped slowly, looking through the dusty panes at a flock of pigeons pecking breadcrumbs. By the third glass, he ordered a plate of fish and chips. He couldn't keep his mind on the food, his thoughts and feelings drifting back to her. She had to be real. He could still feel her in every part of his body. She had to be alive. The teenage boy must be wrong. The food and drink lifted his spirits, leaving him refreshed. The waitress suggested a popular tourist spot, an ancient stone site a few hours away. She scribbled the directions on the back of a napkin. Thanking her, he reached down for the book, accidentally flipping open the cover to the first page. He gasped, startled, bumping into the table and toppling the empty glass. It shattered on the floor.

"Don't worry, sir," the waitress said soothingly, kneeling to sweep up the pieces. "Happens all the time." She didn't see what he was staring at. What had been a blank page only hours before now held twelve words, inscribed in the boldest green ink: *Find the woman with fire hair and she will lead you Home.*

IO

"This place where you are right now,
God circled on a map for you."
—Hafiz

ALLAN SAT IN THE TRUCK, utterly shaken. What did
those words mean? Why was a sentence about a mysterious
woman more unnerving to him than talking to a creature
named Faery? Nervously tapping the bark cover, he
wanted to look inside. He needed more. An explanation
about what the sentence meant. Information about this
woman. Instructions about where he was supposed to go
next. For some reason he couldn't open it. The whole
unsettling experience left him intensely uncomfortable
and anxious. He didn't understand why and didn't
want to. The strange forest book felt like Pandora's
box, threatening consequences he wasn't ready to face.
Visiting the stone circle seemed like a perfect distraction.

Following the young girl's directions, he drove along winding back roads dotted with villages and farmlands, arriving in the late afternoon. Imposing stone sentinels stood guard at the top of a verdant slope. He started to climb out of the truck, then hesitated, impulsively flipping open the book's cover. Blank! The words were gone! Frustrated, turning page after page, edges crumbling onto the seat, nothing. No smudges of green ink. No shadows of letters. Nothing to hint at what he had seen. He slammed the door and headed up to the site. Had he imagined this too? No! The words had been right there. They were emblazoned forever in his brain: *Find the woman with fire hair and she will lead you Home.*

At the top of the hill, he meandered in and out of the expansive stone circle brooding over the blank pages, barely noticing the granite megaliths. How much more of this craziness was he willing to endure? What was real? What was imagined? He felt lost, out of control. He glanced briefly at the interpretive sign recounting legends shrouding the stones, suggesting they served as gathering places for solstice ceremonies and ancient rituals. Touching one of the smooth boulders, a screaming flood of rationality and self-doubt washed over him. Did he honestly think this outlandish quest thing could actually work? That he was cut out for all this mystical crap?

Weary, he headed back to the truck. It was near sunset.

Sitting alone, on a quiet road in rural Ireland, the book beside him, still open, still blank, it all seemed tragically ridiculous. Who was he kidding? If he was chosen for anything, it was for failure. He was as far from hero material as anyone could possibly be. An angry, middle-aged writer, no talent, no job, and no ability to sustain a real relationship. He never should have come.

When he arrived at the B&B, Edna and Patrick O'Sullivan were sitting in the small parlor by the stone fireplace, having finished supper hours ago. Edna immediately sensed something was wrong. She offered him stew. He mumbled an excuse about not feeling well and hurried to his room. Head pounding from the day's events, he found a bottle of aspirin in the medicine cabinet, took two, then went to bed.

He slept fitfully, shards of unsettling images disturbing his rest. Green elfin teenage boys, faces gnarled and pierced, sitting on bar stools, pointing bony fingers. Medusa-like women, hair slithering with red snakes. Ethel Goodwoman sitting on the ground, wearing pink butterfly wings, tugging on his pant leg. But the most frightening image of all was a vast, dark forest. Allan stood trembling in front of a

massive oval mirror embedded in a cold stone mono-
lith, fists clenched, eyes squeezed shut, absolutely
terrified. Behind him, he could feel her, the woman with
fire hair, whispering, urging, open your eyes, Allan, open
your eyes. You must look. He bolted upright, awake. The
ticking bedside clock read 6:17 a.m.

Dressing quickly, he padded quietly down the stairs,
not wanting to see Edna or Patrick. The book, wrapped
in a pillowcase, lay hidden in a bureau drawer.

This time he set out as far from the forest as possible. He walked for miles down a narrow road bordered
on both sides by a crumbling stone wall. A fine rain fell
from the early morning sky, softening everything into a
glistening green. Occasionally someone waved hello: a
little girl with a black and white sheepdog, an old woman
raking leaves. He ignored them. All he could think about
was going back to New York City, back to the things he
knew and understood, back to what felt safe and familiar.
Faery and Ethel Goodwoman, whoever they were, would
have to choose someone else. He simply wasn't up to
the task.

Hungry, he headed back to the cottage. Without
changing his damp clothes, he jumped into the truck and
drove to town.

He found a small restaurant tucked away on a tree-
lined, cobblestoned street, across from a row of quaint

shops selling everything from penny candy to tobacco. A few elderly women in drab woolen coats and knit scarves wandered in and out of stores, while a raucous group of teenagers, smoking cigarettes, milled about.

Inside, Allan sat down at a table, away from the noisy diners who were an interesting mix of tourists and locals. A garden mural decorated the ceiling, with colorful leaves, vines, and petals dripping down the walls. It reminded him of The Alcove, in Manhattan. Though amateur, the art was charming in its own way.

Feeling better, he ordered a hearty breakfast: eggs, bacon, sausage, hash browns, and black pudding. Eating with an unusual intensity, he assured himself that today would be an ordinary day. He'd do some sightseeing, shop a bit, behave like a tourist. Then first thing tomorrow, after a good night's sleep, he'd head to Dublin airport. Buy himself a ticket back to a new life. Find a new job, clean up his apartment, leave anything even remotely weird far behind. The thought soothed him. He glanced around at everyone enjoying their meals. Thank God, he thought, people here seemed perfectly normal.

The small brass bell on the front door tinkled. A woman entered, wearing a velvet cape, forest green, with a hood draped over her head, concealing her face. As she closed the door, he spotted the embroidered design on the back of the cape—a silver tree, three branches with a scattering of gold leaves, and three exposed roots. In the trunk's center, sewn with sparkling thread, glittered a red heart.

Where had he seen that image before? He couldn't remember, yet it was so familiar. As he took a sip of coffee, the woman slipped off her hood, revealing a shock of flowing red hair. He choked, spitting hot liquid all over the tablecloth. The white porcelain cup crashed to the floor.

II

"Do not doubt your own basic goodness.
In spite of all confusion and fear, you are born with a heart
that knows what is just, loving, and beautiful."
—Jack Kornfield

A SMALL COMMOTION ENSUED. The waitress and a few concerned diners rushed over to Allan's table, joined by the restaurant's potbellied owner. They all hovered help-lessly as he coughed uncontrollably. He couldn't stop staring at the figure in green. When she turned around, he collapsed in his chair.

"Sir! Oh, my! Sir?" the waitress prattled, fussing over him like an anxious mother. She was a skinny, puckered-face woman with long red fingernails and too many bracelets. "Oh, my, my, we can't lose an American. Sir? Sir?"

Allan looked up into the face of the caped woman. It was Ethel Goodwoman, her silver-gray hair, loose, covering her shoulders. "Red!" he stammered. "But it was red!"

"Now, Allan," she chuckled as she carefully folded the velvet cape neatly over the back of a chair. "You've got to stop breaking all these dishes." She knelt and picked up jagged pieces of porcelain, all the while assuring the waitress, the owner, and the small crowd that she was, in fact, an old friend and that she would indeed take care of everything. "Really," she insisted, standing up and patting Allan firmly on the back. "He does this kind of thing all the time."

The diners went back to their breakfasts, the skinny waitress and potbellied owner walked off muttering, "Americans."

Ethel Goodwoman tidied up the table, straightening this fork and that butter knife, then ordered a pot of tea. "Perhaps you're drinking a little too much coffee," she said. "Maybe if you had less caffeine."

Still fixated on her hair, he blurted, "I thought it was her, the woman."

"You've got to get beautiful women off your mind, dearie," Ethel Goodwoman chided. "They'll be time enough for that later on."

He stared, mystified. How did she find him? Did she just happen to walk in here? Or had she been following him all along?

"Relax, Allan," she said. "We need to have a little chat."

The waitress set down a fresh pot of tea. Ethel Good-woman politely ordered some toast.

"Chat about what?" he asked, irritated.

"Lots of things. How you're feeling. The next part of the Quest. What to look for when—"

"I'll tell you exactly how I'm feeling," he snapped. "Tired. Frankly, Mrs. Goodwoman, I've had enough questing for a lifetime."

"Really, Allan," she said, a note of impatience in her voice, "I don't see—"

"You don't have to see a damn thing. I'm the one seeing things! Or not seeing things, as the case may be."

Ethel Goodwoman sat back in her chair and looked at Allan intently for a long time. She could see his frustration, his anger, his wanting to flee, all the turmoil that haunted him since he was a small boy.

"No one said this wouldn't be challenging." She affectionately patted his hand. "Your whole life has been challenging, hasn't it? Ever since your mother passed away. Don't you think it's time to—?"

"What are you, my therapist now?" He stood up. "And what does my mother have to do with any of this? I thought this was a mission to save the world!"

Ethel Goodwoman regarded him with great compassion. "You can't save anything, Allan, until you save yourself."

"Look," he replied stiffly, "I don't really know who you are or why you're here. Or why the hell I am. All I know is that I've had all the fairies—with a capital e—and red-haired phantoms and disappearing ink tricks that I can tolerate." Glaring at her, he added, "I've made my decision. I'm leaving. And don't try to stop me." She just sat there, calmly.

"You are a tough one, aren't you?" She smiled because she recognized his fear. The closer one comes to the truth, she thought, the louder the fear cries out. "If you wish to go, Allan, no one is going to interfere. All I ask is that you give me ten minutes to explain."

"Explain what?"

Glancing around the restaurant to make sure no one was listening, she lowered her voice, "Darkside."

"Dark what?"

"Darkside," she repeated quietly. "It's where you have to go to fill in the pages." She gestured to the chair. Reluctantly, he sat.

"Ten minutes. That's it."

"It's not at all as frightening as it sounds," she began.

"What's not frightening?"

"Darkside." The hair stood up on the back of his neck. "After all," she continued, "It's a place we all must travel to. Why without it," she giggled, "there would be no magic in the world a 'tall."

He nibbled mindlessly on a slice of buttered toast. It's hopeless, he thought. The lady is off the deep end.

"There's absolutely nothing wrong with the deep end," she said, "if one's intention is to dive deep."

He paled. Now she could read his thoughts? What next?

"What's next," she replied, "is for you to ask me some of those bothersome questions you have. Get them off your chest so you'll be free to continue. We need you, Allan. We need you to have all your wits about you for the Quest."

Rubbing his forehead, he sighed. "I...I do have questions."

She grinned. "Ask away."

In a grave voice, he began. "The first thing I want to know is why me? I know dozens of people much more qualified for this sort of thing. Take Richard Katz, my best friend in seventh grade. He was always pretending to be a superhero, always the first to the top of the hill. He'd love this stuff. Or my neighbor Assad, a passionate environmentalist and world traveler. Perfect for you guys." Ethel Goodwoman looked at him askance. "Then why in God's name have I been chosen? Why am I the one to complete this quest?"

"Not an unreasonable question a 'tall." She sipped her tea, then said, with conviction, "Because, Allan, you're an exceptionally powerful writer."

A beat or two of silence, then exploding with laughter, barely able to speak, he spit out, "If you and your fairy troops are counting on me to write some sort of bestseller to save the world, you better slit your wings right now!"

Ethel Goodwoman wasn't laughing. In fact, from her somber expression he could see she clearly didn't find any of what he said even the slightest bit amusing.

"This is no joking matter," she insisted. "Our entire planet is at stake." This was spoken with such finality he sat up straighter in the chair. "You were chosen for good reason, Allan. You have special gifts, whether you want to acknowledge them or not. Writing is just one of them." He frowned, shaking his head. Ignoring him, she went on. "You were chosen for other qualities as well. Your intrinsic kindness, for one, and your purity of spirit. And of course, your inherent goodness."

Somewhere in the back of his mind he wanted to make some inane reply. He didn't say a word. He couldn't. He found himself choked up, fighting back an enormous swell of grief. Inherent goodness? Kindness? Purity? No one had ever said anything like that about him. Ever. Women branded him selfish and immature, often much worse. And his father always made it abundantly clear that Allan would never be—could never be—a good, decent, virtuous man. "We've made no mistake, Allan," she said adamantly. "We've been waiting for you. We've waited a long, long time."

He smiled halfheartedly. "I appreciate what you're saying, Mrs. Goodwoman, I really do. Honestly, you've got the wrong man. I'm no hero."

"Oh, but you are, Allan." He looked back at her in disbelief. "Do you think heroes are characters from comic books with bulging muscles and funny capes?" He glanced at her velvet outfit, amused. "Being a hero has nothing at all to do with being physically strong." She paused, allowing him to absorb the words. "Being a hero, Allan, means simply having the courage to live with a tender, open heart." He didn't understand what she meant, and she could see that. "That's why you must go to Darkside." She poured a bit of cream into her tea.

He waited for her to say something more. "That's it?"

The waitress came by to clear some dishes. When she left, Allan asked again, "That's it? That's all you have to say?"

"That's all you need to concern yourself with at the moment. No more questions. Let's move on. Pay close attention because this is important...when you arrive in Darkside you'll need to—"

"I'm not done asking questions," he snapped. He resented the way she dismissed him, as if she had answers for everything, answers that made no sense at all, as if she knew what was best for him. "How do I get to this Darkside place? Where is it? Is it dangerous?"

"I can't tell you that."

"Why not?"

"Because it doesn't work that way."

He snickered. "Then what way does it work, Mrs. Goodwoman? How do I get there? Do you click your ruby heels or sprinkle me with fairy dust?" He defiantly crossed his arms. "And suppose I don't want to go to Darkside. Suppose I decide it's not for me."

"No one can force you, Allan." She paused, stirring the tea. "Darkside must always be your choice. But you know as well as I do that you have unfinished business."

He tensed. "What are you talking about?"

"Your father."

"My father? That's ridiculous. He's dead and buried."

"Not for you."

His chest tightened. "Oh, so now you're going to wave some magic wand and bring him back to life?"

"Don't be childish,' she admonished.

Shoving his chair back, he leapt up. "Don't ever call me childish."

"Allan, please," she said. "Sit down and let's discuss—"

"There's nothing more to discuss," his voice rising. "I'm sick of everyone knowing more than I do, of people appearing and disappearing, of teeny women giving me mysterious instructions and old ladies lecturing me on what it means to be heroic."

The restaurant suddenly grew quiet, everyone watching him. He spread his arms wide, announcing to the curious diners, "If anyone is interested, my name is Allan Quinn Fitzpatrick and I officially proclaim an end to this preposterous quest." He glared at Ethel Goodwoman. "In case you're having trouble reading my mind, let me make myself perfectly clear. I'm going back to New York City. Where everything is bloody sane."

"Oh, my," Ethel Goodwoman said, patting her brow with a green silk handkerchief. "You're turning out to be a bit more problematic than we anticipated."

He grinned. "You're damn right I am."

Outside, a darkened sky threatened thunderstorms. He jumped into the truck, jammed the key into the ignition, slammed down on the acceler- ator and took off, just as the clouds burst.

12

"People have desires. God has plans."
—Anonymous

HE DIDN'T KNOW where he was going. And he didn't care. Maybe he'd drive straight to Dublin Airport, see if there were any night flights back to New York. Gripping the steering wheel, he concentrated on the wet road. Thick rain came down in sheets, heavier than anything since he'd arrived in Ireland. The old rusty wipers splashed back and forth, not clearing the windshield fast enough. He glanced down at the speedometer. Ninety-eight kilometers per hour. About sixty miles per hour. He should probably slow down, the roads were winding and slick, but his mind raced, agitated. Maybe he'd get a hotel in Dublin, spend a few nights. Check out Dublin castle. Fly out in a day or two. But what about the

O'Sullivan's truck? How would he get it back to them? He had a moment of remorse. Edna and Patrick had been perfectly hospitable. Yet the woman got under his skin. The way she watched him, as if she knew something he didn't. Just like Ethel Goodwoman.

You have unfinished business.

"Horseshit." He pressed down on the accelerator. 115 kilometers. Trees flashed by, whipped by wind and rain, the road twisting and turning. Slow down, he told himself again. Cottages sped by, spewing black smoke from their chimneys. 120 kilometers. He focused on Manhattan, what it would feel like to be back in his own apartment. Get some new furniture, buy a few orchids.

Up ahead the road forked. He could barely make out a sign, white lettering, arrow pointing left. *Dublin, 117 kilometers.* That made the most sense. Leave Ireland. Nothing here for him. Work on his resume. Take a few night courses. Find a better job.

Lightning lit up the sky. That's when he saw her. Maybe twenty, thirty yards ahead. A woman, in a long white dress, in the middle of the road. It couldn't be..."Catherine?"

He slammed on the brakes, the old truck skidding wildly on the drenched road. Right, left, right, pumping the brakes, still coming up on her much too fast.

You can't save anything until you save yourself.

For a split second he looked away. Thunder crashed, rattling the truck. An explosion of light. And in the center of the soaked road where she had been standing, a small white deer, eyes glittering through the rain.

"What the...?"

Pounding the brakes, the pedal touched the floorboard. He couldn't slow down, hurtling straight toward the animal. Fifteen yards. Ten yards. Five yards.

Darkside must always be your choice.

Without any hesitation, he jerked the steering wheel to the right. The truck leapt off the road and went barreling down a steep hill. Rocks flew by, branches scraping against windows. Clutching the wheel, he tried desperately to gain control, the shabby seatbelt barely holding him. The truck smashed into a small boulder, bounding five feet into the air. He screamed as it slammed to the ground, nothing stopping its wild trajectory down the hill. Dizzy, something trickling down his cheek, metal screeching, tearing, shredding. He lifted his head just in time to see, rushing madly towards him at a frightening speed, a wall of imposing evergreens, the truck dead set on a collision course with a massive forest.

"Oh, God!" Then everything went black.

13

"Turn your wounds into wisdom."
—Oprah Winfrey

JAMMED BETWEEN TWO towering trees, the truck's front end lay crushed in a twisted mass of wrecked steel. In a daze, Allan somehow managed to shove open a door and stumble out. A thin trail of blood outlined his cheek. Trying to walk, he fell, then stood up again, shaking violently. He touched his face and head, feeling for eyes, nose, mouth and chin, hair matted with blood, and a large gash on his forehead. "I'm okay," he repeated desperately. "I'm okay."

In front of him loomed the edge of a vast forest. Everything looked gray and foreboding. He lunged forward but the effort was too much, collapsing to the ground.

He had no idea how long he lay there. When he heard someone calling his name, he tried with every ounce of strength to sit up. He heard his name again. A woman's voice. "Allan," she called. "Allan."

With tremendous effort, he stood up, scanning the woods in front of him. A flash of red. "Catherine?"

There she was, a few yards away, white lace dress, red hair loose and wild. "Allan." Then she turned around and disappeared into the woods.

"Wait!" he cried out. "Catherine!" Lurching forward, his body throbbing, he followed her, reeling like a drunkard. When he reached the spot where she had

been standing, he saw a narrow path of trampled leaves that stretched out before him. He thought he heard her. "Catherine," he cried weakly. "Wait. Please!"

Stumbling, his body pumping every bit of adrenaline it could muster, he followed the sound of footsteps, disappearing deeper and deeper into the woods.

He never noticed the splintered wooden sign nailed to a pine tree that stood at the entrance to the forest. Seventeen letters carved into its weathered surface: WELCOME TO DARKSIDE.

PART THREE

Transformation

"The time has come.
Do not be afraid.
The time You have always known about.
The time that sages and scriptures have prophesized.

You who have never been a hero
Must be one Now.
You who have never saved a world
Must save one Now.
You do not need the strength of a hundred lions.
Just the courage of one heart.
You do not need the mind of a hundred wisemen.
Just the faith of one child.

You who have wished so long for meaning,
Who have prayed so long for purpose,
A True Quest.
You are the Chosen One.
Remember. Please, remember."

—The Ancient Book of Fae

14

"It's not forgetting that heals, it's remembering."
—Amy Greene

WHEN HE COULDN'T RUN ANYMORE, he slowed to a clumsy, stumbling pace. Exhausted, his vision blurry, all he could think about was her. All he could see were the words in the book: *Find the woman with fire hair and she will lead you Home.*

He tripped, tumbling to the ground, lay there panting, then dragged himself to his feet and continued on the path. Finally, after what felt like miles, he fell for the last time. He wanted to get up, wanted to pursue her, but he couldn't even lift his hand. Exhausted, he slipped into a dark sleep.

Raindrops on his skin brought him back to consciousness. He could feel them. Moist and cool, tapping his eyelids and cheeks. Focusing his groggy attention on the sensation, he noticed they weren't droplets at all. His face was being slathered. It occurred to him he was being licked.

His eyes shot open. Peering down at him, a blur of soft white, was the face of a wild doe, the color of snow, with liquid brown eyes fringed in long pale lashes. She was licking him, washing away the blood. He lay there, motionless, more out of fascination than weakness, holding his breath. He had never been this close to a wild animal. And he had never in his life seen a white doe.

When he finally exhaled, she backed away. Don't go, he thought. You're beautiful. She blinked and he heard a gentle *thank you*.

He glanced around, certain that someone had said the words aloud. No one was there except the doe who stood perfectly still a few feet away. Being careful not to disturb the animal, he sat up very slowly. She continued to watch him. He noticed how small she was, only about three feet high, with a long slender neck and delicate legs. Then she scraped her left front hoof on the ground. *This is Darkside.*

Puzzled, he glanced at the trees surrounding him, wondering why he would think such an odd thing. The doe shook her head vigorously, as if she had a long flowing mane. *This is the place all healing begins.*

Why was he thinking these strange things? The doe took a step backward, then a step forward. *This is the place all Truth is born.*

An odd feeling crept over him. He glanced anxiously at the animal who never stopped watching him, almost too embarrassed to admit his thought. Could the deer be communicating with him?

He examined her more intently. How in the world could he even consider such an outrageous notion? The doe's velvety soft ears perked up in alertness. *Do not be afraid* flashed through his mind. *Whatever happens, do not be afraid.* Then, in one swift graceful motion, she bounded off, flying across the narrow-trodden path. Utterly bewildered, Allan watched her disappear into the tangled woods.

Carefully, he stood up, afraid he might still be too weak. He noticed a renewed strength in his legs and arms. The sleep must have done him good. He touched his cheek and head, feeling for the fresh wounds. His skin felt soft, moist—no bumps, scabs, or gashes. Had she somehow healed him? Was there something medicinal in her saliva? His stomach rumbled. How long had he been asleep? Hours? Days? He took a few steps. A thick branch lay across the path. It would work as a walking stick. He picked it up and continued on his way.

His breathing deepened and relaxed, and he felt

a surge of vitality, an aliveness, like a boy out on an adventure. His logical mind rebelled, insisting he should be worried, concerned. He had just been in a horrible accident, and now was lost in the middle of a strange forest. Yet despite those thoughts, he continued to feel stronger and more enthusiastic. *This is the place all healing begins.* He smiled at the absurdity of a wild animal talking to him telepathically, telling him this forest was "DARKSIDE!" The place Ethel Goodwoman had spoken about. The next place he was supposed to go on the quest! Every hair on his body stood on end. Every fiber in him wanted to run. *Do not be afraid. Whatever happens, do not be afraid.*

He concentrated on the surroundings. Massive trees towering above, sunlight peeking through a dense canopy of leaves, a profusion of lacy ferns sprouting from rocks, roots, and soil. Walking briskly, his fear dissipating, he followed the path up over a small rise. When he reached the top, he spotted a small cabin, made of logs and stone. Dark smoke floated lazily above the chimney. An open shed nearby housed a tall pile of chopped wood. Prodding the ground with the tip of the stick, stomach growling, he edged his way slowly down the hill. Whoever lived there was sure to help.

As he reached the bottom, the cabin door opened. Standing there, smiling, was the woman with fire hair.

15

"All love stories are tales of beginnings."
—Megan O'Rourke

HE STOOD ON THE PORCH, stunned. She was even more beautiful than he remembered, her hair, the color of rubies, flowing down to her waist.

"Would you like to come in?" she asked. "I put the kettle on for tea."

He nodded, unable to speak, and followed. Being this close to her overwhelmed him. All he wanted to do was sweep her into his arms. He was absolutely and utterly in love. They walked inside.

Light streamed through an array of paned windows. The walls, hewn from rounded cedar logs, gave the room a sweet forest scent. A beamed ceiling looked down on a collection of rustic furniture—a grainy, brown leather couch with a multicolored fringed wool blanket tossed casually across the back, two overstuffed, suede chairs, and a wrought iron coffee table made of recycled glass and wood. The stone fireplace had a wide oak mantle displaying wax candles of different shapes and sizes, polished stones and seashells, and a fist-sized piece of raw, glittering quartz. She led him into a small kitchen, pine shelves lined the walls, draped with strings of dried

herbs, glass jars filled with crumbled leaves, twigs, and seeds. A vase of fresh cut flowers brightened the round oak table. Above a white porcelain sink, a window, framed by pale yellow curtains, looked out into the woods. She gestured for him to take a seat while she made the tea.

"These herbs are from an alder tree," she said softly, pouring the dark brown liquid into a ceramic mug. "They'll help with your healing and allow you to sleep."

He thanked her, wrapping his fingers around the warm mug, the spicy aroma relaxing him even more. He sipped slowly.

"It's good," he said, gazing at her. He didn't want to blink, afraid she would disappear again. She sat there calmly, exuding a peacefulness he had never seen in a person before. For a split second, he had the disturbing thought he might be dreaming. "Are you—"

"Real?" she laughed, her voice rich and melodic. "Don't I look real?"

"More real than anyone I've ever known."

He could see she knew it was a compliment. In fact, he could see that she wasn't bothered at all by his puppy-like adoration. She didn't seem the least bit unbalanced by it. The odd thing was, she didn't seem unbalanced by anything.

"I have so many questions," he said. "I don't know where to begin." She waited patiently. "They think...they think you're dead. Your father..."

She took a few moments before answering. "Sometimes," she said, her voice laced with sadness, "we must do things that may cause pain in the people we love. Because there is a greater purpose." She lifted her scalloped, lace collar, revealing a small, round shimmering pin. "Sometimes," she continued, "we must surrender to the Quest."

He gasped at the sight of the engraved golden circle. The same design on Ethel Goodwoman's pin, the same design embroidered on the back of her cape.

"The tree," he exclaimed. He looked up at her. "It's the exact same tree."

"I know." She let her collar gracefully fall back, hiding the pin once more. "Only those of us who have accepted the Quest wear one."

Those of us? "But I thought..."

"You were the only one?" She smiled kindly. "There are many others on the Quest."

Confused and disturbed, he asked, "Then why did they tell me I was chosen? Why am I needed if everyone else is doing the same thing?"

She grew more serious. "The Quest is different for each one of us," she said. "We each seek the answers we need. Yours is to fill the pages and bring back the sacred branches."

He was shocked at her knowledge. "How did you—?"

"Darkside is the place all Truth is born."

He fell back against the chair, trying to make sense of everything happening, everything she was telling him.

They sat together, quietly, for what seemed like a long time. He couldn't remember ever feeling this at ease with such a beautiful woman. Finally, he asked, "What about you, Catherine? What are you looking for?"

"That's not important," she replied.

"I'd like to know."

She stood up and went to the sink. "Allan," she began, her back to him, "all of us were born with a purpose, a mission." She spun around, a fierceness flashing in her green eyes. "It's not important what I have come to find. What you need to know is that it's your innermost gifts and greatest strengths that will determine the path of your journey."

Listening carefully, he wondered what those gifts truly were. Ethel Goodwoman insisted he'd been chosen for his kindness and purity, even for his writing, though he still found that explanation difficult to accept. There was so much more he wanted to know, so many questions to ask.

"You must be very tired," she said, touching his shoulder and he felt an overwhelming exhaustion. "Let me show you your room." She helped him stand, her hands small and soft, yet her grip unusually strong. He looked at her more closely, wondering about her age. She had the innocence of a girl barely twenty, yet the wisdom and grace of someone much older. As she walked beside him, holding his arm, he had to fight a powerful impulse to pull her to his chest and kiss her.

"It's a simple room," she said, opening the door to a sparsely furnished bedroom. A single bed with an intricately carved headboard made from silver birch. An exquisite handmade quilt covered the bed, with an embroidered design in the center, of a small child standing amid a circle of trees. Beside the bed a nightstand held an antique lamp. Nestled in the corner, by the window draped in a sheer white curtain, sat a small wooden desk and chair. "You'll sleep well here," she said, and then surprised him with a light kiss on his cheek. "Tomorrow is an important day for you, Allan." As she closed the door, she added, "Good luck."

Mesmerized, the kiss burning his skin, he barely heard anything she said. He wanted this woman more than he ever wanted anyone in his life. He considered rushing after her. But he was hesitant. He'd never encountered a woman like this. Usually, he was good at reading what women wanted, at least initially. He imagined the ideal fantasy: knocking lightly on her bedroom door, he calls out her name. Without any hesitation, she invites him in. Sitting on the bed, moonlight streaming through the small window, she smiles. Urged on by passion, he moves closer, barely able to contain his longing. But then she raises her hand. He stops, unable to move and abruptly, against his will, the fantasy changes.

"I know the depth of what you're feeling," she says softly. "I feel it too." A thrilling rush of excitement spills over him. He tries again to move closer, to touch her but can't, as if an invisible barrier stands between them. "This bond we have is real," she continues. "In Celtic spiritual tradition it's known as *anam cara*. Soul friends."

Friends. He didn't want to hear that. He desperately wanted so much more. Dejected, he sat down on the edge of his own bed, the vision gone. Fire still coursed through his veins, insisting he go to her now, right now, that she could change her mind; that it made no sense, a woman this alluring, this exquisite, not sleeping beside him. Yet somehow, even though this was all in his imagination, he knew she was right. He knew that despite what every cell in his physical body hungered for, they weren't meant to be lovers, at least not now. Half-heartedly, he undressed and slipped under the covers, tossing and turning, trying to understand this uncomfortable new-found honesty. Finally drifting off to sleep, one last thought occurred to him: *Darkside is the place all Truth is born.*

16

"A good traveler has no fixed plans
and is not intent upon arriving."
—Lao-Tzu

AWAKENED BY THE NOISY chatter of birds, Allan sat up, feeling an extraordinary sense of vitality, wondering if it was the potent tea Catherine had given him yesterday. He dressed quickly, deciding it was more likely the intoxicating effect she had on his entire being. He simply refused to believe there could be no possibility of romance.

Eager to see her, he hurried into the living room, then the kitchen. She wasn't there. "Catherine?" he called out. The cabin felt deserted. Stopping in front of her bedroom door, he tentatively knocked. "Catherine?" No response. He opened the door. The room, only slightly larger than his, had a double bed with a beautiful stained glass headboard and footboard. The window was partially open, a cool breeze wafting in through white lace curtains, and the bed neatly made with a patchwork quilt of blues and greens. Perplexed, he walked around, searching for some clue. An oval mirror, framed in pewter, hung over an old oak bureau. The room had a simple yet rustic elegance. Feeling like a thief, he quietly opened the top drawer. Empty. He opened the others— all empty.

He went back into the kitchen. Everything looked the same as the night before. Glass jars filled with herbs. A wood-burning stove, still warm, with a copper teakettle sitting on top. And the same tall vase of flowers in the center of the table. A creepy feeling came over him. He dismissed it. She must have gone somewhere, maybe an early morning hike in the woods. Confused, wandering through the cabin, he wasn't sure what to do. He ended up outside, and sat down on the back porch steps, wondering when he would see her again.

He remained there for a long time, waiting for her to return. A mounting anxiety nagged him. "Tomorrow is an important day," she'd said last night. Had she wished him good night or good luck? He couldn't remember.

Why hadn't she waited for him to wake up? Why hadn't she left him a note? Why had she run off?

Hungry and irritated, he went into the kitchen but couldn't find anything to eat. Back in his room, he lay down on the bed, fighting a growing depression. Maybe there's a town nearby, he rationalized. Maybe she went shopping for supplies. When he spotted the book from the forest sitting on the desk, he paled.

He knew he left the book at the O'Sullivan's, hidden in the drawer. How had it gotten here? Ignoring his own question, he crept closer. Whatever happens, he reminded himself, do not be afraid. He lifted the cover.

The pages were blank.

"Damn!" With all the weirdness going on, he fully expected something to be written there. A word, a riddle, a clue! Nobody told him this quest would be so baffling.

Exasperated, he grabbed the book and headed out. No point hanging around. Summoning up a more positive outlook, he decided to go explore.

Determined, he set out on the path, listening to the dry leaves crunching beneath his shoes. Abruptly he stopped. Where was he going? What was he supposed to do? He hadn't the faintest idea. In fact, he didn't even know where he was. He sat down on a large, flat rock to think, the book on his lap. Trailing his fingers across the nubby cover and sap-stained spine, he wondered why he was bothering to carry it at all. Then it occurred to him that maybe he wasn't using the book correctly. Everyone kept telling him how he needed to fill the pages and yet it seemed he couldn't fill a paragraph's worth. And the one sentence that had appeared didn't even stay. Maybe he needed to treat the book more like—he searched his mind for the right words—more like a touchstone, like a magic lantern! An image of Ethel Goodwoman popped into his head—an elderly genie bursting out of the book in a puff of smoke, a green velvet turban wrapped around her head. He chuckled. Maybe he needed to ask the book for help, sort of pray for an answer. It felt a bit silly but when he considered everything he'd been through, he knew he had nothing to lose. Picturing the book in his mind's eye, he asked for some sort of direction. Perhaps he needed to be more specific, ask for a map. A map with arrows, pointing the way. Then he could follow it until he found whatever he was supposed to find. He silently asked again for direction and opened the book.

To his tremendous disappointment, the page remained blank. He stared unwaveringly, refusing to give

up. Then something blurred before his eyes, a faint blotch of green that seemed to grow larger. He concentrated more intently. The green spot grew darker, wider, elongating, forming into words. A few seconds passed, then seven words, in bold green ink: *Accept Uncertainty and Life Will Be Good.*

"What kind of direction is that?" He threw his hands up in frustration, knocking the book to the ground. "I know that one already!" Annoyed, he wondered how advice from a crumpled cocktail napkin could possibly have anything important to do with this quest. He glared down at the book by his feet, kicking it lightly. It was starting to feel more like an adversary than ally.

"Oh, all right," he grumbled, picking it up and plopping it back on his lap. "I'll accept the damn uncertainty!" He flipped open the cover again hoping he could discover some deeper meaning. Once again, the page was blank.

The lunacy of the situation—praying to a pile of bark and sap, ink appearing and disappearing, listening to cocktail napkins, made him burst out laughing. He patted the book affectionately and considered his options.

There was only one real path, the one that lay before him, the one that had led him here. "Might as well." With the book nestled securely under his arm, he strode off, grinning.

17

"When nothing is sure, everything is possible."
—Margaret Drabble

HE HADN'T GONE VERY FAR, perhaps a mile or so, when he heard the sound. He thought it was a bird singing. As he got closer, he realized the sounds were words, strange words he couldn't understand—a melodic, haunting song. His first thought was of Catherine. As he listened, the voice sounded much too young. He crept closer until he spotted a girl, about ten or eleven years old, long braided hair, singing and dancing in the middle of the woods.

He knelt beside a small boulder, not wanting to startle her. It appeared she was singing to a felled tree, a massive oak that looked newly cut. The slice, smooth and clean, obviously done by the hand of men. The stump itself was perhaps five feet in diameter. The tree had crashed down a few feet away.

The young girl was singing in a different language. Allan thought he recognized the rhythm and cadence as Gaelic, reminding him of lullabies his mother sang to him as a child. Although he couldn't understand a word, he could feel their meaning. The little girl seemed to be pleading, her pure sweet voice laced with sadness. She moved slowly, gracefully, eyes closed, head back in a pose of abandon, her small hand lightly stroking the severed surface. Sometimes she'd brush her fingers along the body of the felled trunk, always moving, swaying, singing. Allan watched, transfixed, wanting more than anything to know what she was saying.

"I'd be happy to translate."

Startled, he whirled around. Faery hovered right in front of him.

"Where have you—?" Before he could finish the question, Faery touched her feather-light finger to his lips. Then, fluttering even closer, she began softly singing in English:

"Gentle tree, I cry for thee
Your beauty bold, your wisdom old
Oh, gentle tree, please grow for me
I sing thy praises, I sing for thee."

Allan turned back to the young girl. Over and over she sang this haunting song. And over and over, Faery softly sang the words:

"Gentle tree, I cry for thee
Your beauty bold, your wisdom old
Oh, gentle tree, please grow for me
I sing thy praises, I sing for thee."

Faery stopped singing and only the young girl's innocent voice could be heard. She began to cry but her chanting would not cease, nor the graceful movements of her dance. Allan fought the sorrow welling up inside. A great melancholy swept over him.

It had been a majestic tree. The ancient Celts beloved *duir,* a mighty oak, worshipped as king of the forest, a sacred symbol of immortal strength and fertility, its powerful branches abundant with dark green leaves and golden acorns. A tree that had stood for more than two hundred years.

He tried to make sense of it. He knew all the reasons:

We need the wood for houses and schools. We need the wood for hospitals and books. We need the wood. Yet his sorrow remained, logic unable to wash it away. The magnificent tree was dead. The young girl continued chanting her song:

> *"Gentle tree, I cry for thee*
> *Your beauty bold, your wisdom old*
> *Oh, gentle tree, please grow for me*
> *I sing thy praises, I sing for thee."*

She sang and danced for hours. Rooted, he couldn't move, mesmerized by the enchanting spell. Faery sat quietly on his shoulder, nestled comfortably in the crook of his neck.

Soon the forest grew eerily quiet. Birds ceased chattering, leaves stopped rustling, insects stopped buzzing, and branches no longer creaked or swayed. Nothing but perfect stillness. The young girl's words stinging the silence. She continued her ancient paean. The words hung like crystals in the motionless air. Allan felt his pulse quicken, his skin tingling. Something was happening.

The severed trunk began to vibrate, levitate, float higher and higher above the ground. Righting itself in midair, the enormous oak hovered over the base. The young girl never changed her sound or her tone or her rhythm. Over and over, she chanted the solemn words.

"Gentle tree, I cry for thee
Your beauty bold, your wisdom old
Oh, gentle tree, please grow for me
I sing thy praises, I sing for thee."

The trunk landed powerfully on its base, the explosive sound reverberating through the forest. Allan watched in utter amazement, as the tree, now completely upright and whole began to sway, ever so slightly in the wind. Black and white magpies and spotted woodpeckers landed on its lush branches, blue jays and robins gathered to build their nests, squirrels nibbled on acorns, and infinitesimal troops of ants trailed up and down the gray, fissured bark.

The young girl stopped singing. For a moment she stood motionless, surveying the lofty oak. Content, she sighed, then skipped away.

"It's a miracle," he said, his voice filled with awe.

Faery—whom he had completely forgotten about—fluttered nearby. "No Allan, it's not a miracle at all," she said. "It's the First Sacred Branch." He looked at her in wonderment. She began to fade, sparkling in the sunlight, her disembodied voice trailing behind: *"Witness Life and Praise All Things."*

He looked around for the ancient book. It lay right by his feet. Kneeling, he carefully lifted the cover. "Behold!" the fresh green ink announced in cursive glory, *"The Power of Praise!"*

18

"I will sing to you at every moment,
I will praise you with every breath."

—Psalm 104

PAGE AFTER PAGE FILLED with words, crowded with green inked paragraphs, underlined sentences, all in a swirling calligraphy. Allan sat cross legged in the woods, enthralled.

"I did it! I filled the pages!"

Faery suddenly appeared, perched on his knee. "Now don't get carried away," she cautioned. "It's not yet time to read."

"Not time? What else do I have to do?"

She smiled, a mischievous glint in her eyes. "Practice."

"Practice? Practice what?"

"Praising!" she sang. "That's what the First Sacred Branch is all about."

He thought of the young girl and the miracle he had

just seen. "You mean you want me to sing and dance in Gaelic?"

Faery giggled. "No, of course not. Everyone praises in their own way. Whatever feels good."

He settled back against the boulder. She wanted him to compliment things? The idea seemed silly. "Is this really part of the quest?" he asked. She nodded enthusiastically. "You mean to tell me that this...this praising thing is going to save the earth?"

Faery crossed her arms and smiled. "The idea, Allan, is not to save the earth—"

"But you explicitly instructed me on the plane."

"Savor Her instead. Praise is the rain and sun and food She needs. Praise Her in everything you do."

He leaned closer to Faery and said, shyly, "You're very sweet, you know. And really quite beautiful." She blushed, giggling. "Is that what you mean?'

"Perfect!"

He stood up, noticing a nearby cluster of glistening leaves. "You're lovely," he said, then glanced back over his shoulder to see if Faery was watching. She was already gone. "Very lovely," he repeated, gently stroking one shiny leaf. He picked up the book and followed the path. He stopped in front of a nubby spruce. "You're beautiful," he said, and swept his fingers across the soft pine needles.

On and on he walked, complimenting a newborn fern

here and a blade of grass there. He praised the mushroom peeking out of the dark soil, admiring the moon white stem and umbrella top. He could picture Faery sitting beneath it to get out of the rain. He spotted a patch of moss growing on the side of a rock. "How green, like emeralds." Noticing the earth tones of the rock itself, he said, "And you're a handsome fellow as well." He slowed his pace, unable to pass even the tiniest yellow flower peeking from behind a branch. He praised the stately trees surrounding him, wondering what type they were and if he needed to know their names. Faery reappeared; this time balanced precariously on the tip of a wispy branch above his head.

"We need no names in the Hidden Kingdom," she told him. "We know who we are. All we need is Praise."

He stopped and praised the mighty boulder standing guard beside the rushing river. He praised the river, too, and though he could not see them, all the creatures that lived within it. "You're exquisite," he chanted again and again, the beauty touching him deeply. By the time he reached the cabin, his heart fuller and more tender, a great stillness enveloped him, his senses awakened, connecting him, profoundly, to everything.

When he entered, he didn't notice the cabin was still deserted. He headed straight to his room. He knew it would soon be time to read the book and learn more about this amazing thing called Praise. He was surprised to

find a small leather journal and pen on the desk by the window, a note beside it, the handwriting loose and free. "To help you grow. Love, Catherine." He was overcome with gratitude for absolutely everything. For Catherine not abandoning him after all, and for Faery always appearing at the right time. And for discovering, today, the first sacred branch. He touched the smooth leather, then opened the book, glad to have a place to write things down, to remember more vividly all that was happening.

His stomach growled, making him acutely aware of his growing hunger. He took the journal and walked into the kitchen. A blue ceramic pot sat on the stove beside a warm loaf of dark bread. He lifted the pot's cover, inhaling the delicious aroma of a hearty vegetable stew.

Eating slowly, he began seeing everything around him in a new way, as if his eyesight were keener, his sense of observation more acute. He noticed the young green shoots sprouting from the twigs inside the glass jars on the shelves. He noticed the graceful movement of the kitchen curtain as it billowed with each puff of wind.

Opening his new journal to the first page, he began writing. He wrote for pages about his old notions of praise and how wrong he had been all his life, thinking that praise belonged only to red-faced preachers in stiff collars or to choirs of religious men and women wearing satin robes. He put the pen down momentarily and looked around the room, wondering whether he was supposed to praise non-living things as well. Like the glazed ceramic bowl that held his steaming soup or the wooden ladle lying in the sink. Then he remembered what Faery said in the forest just before she disappeared. *Witness Life And Praise All Things.* So, he praised the ladle and the tree it came from and the porcelain sink and the stack of dishes sitting on the shelf. It felt good to praise. And then he wrote, "It's much simpler than I thought, this thing called Praise. It's just the willingness to honor, to celebrate the preciousness of life."

Back in his room, eager to begin reading, he carefully opened the sacred book, half expecting the words to be gone. Finding the text still there, he flipped quickly through the pages. Every single one was filled. He wondered how there would be room for the other sacred branches as well. That didn't matter now. He was too excited to start reading. He turned back to page one: "Praise is the reason that all things exist," the book revealed. "It is the basis of life on earth. Without Praise, life simply could not be." He paused, considering the weight of that statement. "All things exist *to be* Praised. All things exist *as* Praise." The concept intrigued him. "The Hidden Kingdom is rooted in Praise. Praise is not an idea or a philosophical notion. Praise *is* the Universal Seed."

He stayed up late into the night, reading, soaking in

Praise

Witness Life and Praise All Things.

the truths like soil permeated with rain. As he read, he grew hungry for more. As he read more, he grew satiated. Page after page, the words poured out, all focused on one central theme. "We of the Ancient Realm are beings of Praise. Our mission, our purpose on earth is simply To Praise All Things."

He thought about Faery and smiled. "We were created before humans existed. We are the overflow from the Divine. Our only purpose is to celebrate the wonder of the physical world, to honor and revere all that is alive."

He stopped reading, letting the words wash over him. When he was ready, he continued: "We are here to applaud the miracle of the bud and the majesty of the rose. We are here to leap with holy delight before the glory of the spider and the wonder of the whale. We are here to bow in absolute appreciation before the rolling thunder and the dawn. This has been our mission since time began. Praise is not simply what we do. It is who we are: Living Beings of Praise."

He set the book aside on the bed and lay down. He didn't understand why the words were affecting him this way. He thought again of Faery, remembering the pained look on her face when she said, "We are dying, Allan. All of us. We are dying."

He stood up and began to pace, disturbed, wondering what she really meant, gripped with a burning desire not to fail her, not to let her down. He went back to the book and read on: "When humankind came to be, it was assumed they too would carry out this purpose. It was assumed they too would celebrate the life around them. But something began to happen. Time passed and the praising ceased. The forgetting of this Truth," the book told him, "is one of the great causes of Earth's new sickness. Praise is what She needs, what She hungers for, what makes Her thrive. All things living must be Praised."

The magnitude of the words astounded him. He wondered if they were genuinely true, if this ancient book held power—real power. He imagined rejection and scorn from friends hearing these newfound truths.

He gently placed his palms on the warm page, recalling the haunting song of the young girl dancing in the forest, and the miracle of the tree. His soul knew the power emanating within these truths was real.

"We can no longer work alone," the book said. "The Ancient Realm needs help. We need humankind to remember. To remember why they are here. To reclaim the Universal Seed. To reclaim the glory and beauty and power of Praise."

By the time he fell asleep that night he had read and reread the entire book. He slept with it open on his chest, sheltering his heart. He slept as the sun rose. He slept as the day went on. It was a healing sleep. A sleep of learning and assimilating. Every cell in his body was remembering. It was a sleep of the innocent.

When he woke, it was almost night. For a moment he wasn't sure where he was. When he felt the gentle weight of the book on his chest and looked outside his window, he knew. The moon, an enormous pale, silver disk, glowed in the twilight sky. He sat up in bed watching it for the longest time; beams of moonlight illuminating the room, casting pearly white shadows on the windowsill, on the walls, on the smooth wooden floor.

He realized that he hadn't felt this content since he was a small child. To no one in particular, he murmured, "Thank you." Glancing down at the book, he added, "Praise be to God." He thought no one was listening. He was wrong. The Hidden Kingdom heard him. And a wisp of moonlight touched his bed in silent gratitude.

19

"Sometimes I go about pitying myself,
while all the time I am being carried
on great winds across the sky."
—Chippewa song

HE WOKE JUST AFTER DAWN. Catherine's laughter made him jump out of bed. She'd come back! He had so much to tell her. Tucking his wrinkled shirt into his pants, he combed his fingers through his hair in an attempt to look decent.

Rushing out of the room, he had no idea what time it was. He must have slept for more than sixteen hours. He just wanted to be with Catherine.

The laughter came from outside the cabin. Excited, he pulled open the front door, a broad smile on his face, but his happiness instantly shattered. Catherine was passionately kissing another man.

He fell back against the door, as if pierced by a sharp blade, anger threatening to engulf him.

They didn't notice him. The man was tall and pale, with long blonde hair Allan couldn't see his face because Catherine was pressed against him, his fingers buried in her hair. Swallowing hard, fighting back an explosive rage, he wanted to grab the man and choke the life from him. He wanted to bludgeon him with a rock until his skull split open. The hateful images bombarded him, adrenaline pumping madly. As he took a shaky step forward, Catherine looked up.

"Allan!" When he saw her face, her beautiful emerald eyes, a pain tore through his chest. He bolted, running off into the woods. "Allan!" she cried out. "Wait! Please!"

He ran as fast as he could, trying to outrace the despair. Why? Why? It was all too much. To be led to a woman like Catherine. A woman more magnificent than any he'd ever known. To be led to her by these strange mystical circumstances. To live in her house. To eat the food she cooked for him. And then to be horribly betrayed.

Rage and grief battled for dominance. He railed against God and against everything he'd ever known. Then he sobbed like a little boy.

Finally, feeling emptied, hollow, he sat down on the ground. A terrible coldness gripped his heart. He sat that way for a long time, until Faery appeared by his feet. He noticed her but didn't bother to lift his head. She smiled shyly.

Inching closer, she flapped her feather light wings, lifting her body onto the petal of a nearby lily. Settling comfortably, she pulled her knees to her chest and said, in great earnestness, "Things will work out, Allan." She smiled, encouragingly. "They always do."

He snorted, grabbing a handful of pebbles. "Aren't you the eternal optimist."

"Op-ti-mist?" she repeated clumsily. "What's that?"

He tossed the rocks. "You know, the glass is always half full, there's a damn silver lining in every damn cloud, that sort of horsesh—" He caught himself. "That sort of stuff."

"Hmmm…" Faery replied thoughtfully. "Then everyone is optimist?"

"An optimist. It's a noun. And no, not everyone is an optimist. Especially if they're part Jewish." The humor, of course, eluded her.

Faery edged carefully up to the very tip of the petal. "What else can they be then?" she asked sincerely.

"A pessimist. Like me. Pess-i-mist. We believe in Murphy's Law—if things can break or die, they will."

"But all things break and die," Faery replied cheerfully, "and all things grow again. How can anyone be sad about that?"

"You know, Faery, I gotta admire you. You're always so damn upbeat." Mumbling under his breath, he added, "wish I could be more like that."

"You can," she chirped.

"How? By sprouting little wings?"

"Oh, no. You can't sprout wings," she said adamantly. "You're human."

He shot her another sour look. "No kidding."

"But you can still be more like us. All you have to do is learn what we know."

He stood up to stretch his legs, then picked up a long branch and began absently poking the dirt. "Sounds too much like another mission. Sorry, only one quest per lifetime, thank you."

Delicately, she leapt off the petal and fluttered up to him. "It's simple," she insisted.

"Faery," he said, "nothing is simple with you."

"It is, Allan, I promise. All you have to do is learn The Attitude."

He broke the dead branch across his knee and used it to scratch his back. "The attitude?"

"Yes!" she said enthusiastically. "It's what we live by. What everything alive lives by, what everything on earth lives by."

He sat down on a log. "What everything on earth lives by? What is it—some kind of weird New Age philosophy?"

She thought about that for a moment, her forehead wrinkling into infinitesimal lines. "Well...no, it's not a philosophy. It's just...just The Attitude." Allan cocked his head. "You know, the way we look at everything—The Attitude." She could see he was still confused. "Hope, Possibility, Growth!" she exclaimed.

"Excuse me?"

"That's the Attitude. It's as old as the earth itself. Hope, Possibility, Growth."

It all sounded a bit too Hallmark for him. He could just picture the greeting card. On the cover, a bright yellow daisy with a pink frilly Tinkerbell hovering above it. Open it up and it says `Wishing you hope, possibility and growth!'

"Try it," she suggested. "You'll see."

"See what?"

"How much better you'll start to feel." She was beaming at him now. He could see she believed wholeheartedly in every word.

"Look, Faery," he began, "I suppose if I were you and all I had to do every day was flit from one daisy to another, I'd be deliriously happy too."

Her smile vanished. "Allan Quinn Fitzpatrick," she said sharply, putting her dainty hands on her hips, "that is not what we do all day. We work very hard, all the time." She gestured to the nearby brook and to the patch of wildflowers a few feet away and to the magnificent forest surrounding them. "Look at all this. *This* is our work. *This* is the reason we exist."

He remembered last night's pages. *Living Beings of Praise.*

He looked over at her, hovering so passionately, then looked around at what she was pointing to. A crystal-clear brook gurgled nearby. Polished black rocks poked through the water's surface. Dark brown water bugs with long spindly legs skated gracefully across. He noticed the wildflowers, radiant in speckled sunlight, their pink, white and lavender flowers bursting from the stems. Orange and yellow butterflies danced from petal to petal, red headed cardinals chirped in the pine branches above his head. Even the log he sat on was covered with a splendid velvety moss. It was really quite an idyllic setting.

"This is our work," she repeated passionately, "and we can do it because of The Attitude. Hope, Possibility—"

"Growth," he interrupted, finishing her sentence. "I know."

It's not that he wanted to argue. It just seemed simplistic and superficial to him, too Disneyesque. Faery fluttered near his ear. "It's as real as your despair."

"Yeah, Faery, I'm sure you believe that."

"What's *your* attitude?" she asked.

"What do you mean?"

"Your attitude. About life. About everything."

He considered the question. What was his attitude about life? What was his core perspective? How did he generally feel?

"You really want to know?" She nodded eagerly. With a twisted grin he replied, "Despair, Impossibility, Stagnation. That's the Fitzpatrick Way."

Faery didn't think that was funny. She screwed her little face up into a sad frown. "I'm sorry," she said. "It must be very hard to live like that."

He shrugged. "Yeah, well, it ain't much fun."

She fluttered over and landed lightly on his shoulder.

"Why not try ours? Just try it, Allan. It can't hurt, can it?"

He tilted his head to get a better look. There she sat, this minuscule bright-eyed woman, working diligently to help him feel better. He softened. "Okay, Faery," he said with a half-smile. "I'll try it."

She clapped her hands, giddy with delight. "Oh, rosebud!"

"I have just one question," he said.

She stood up and meticulously dusted herself off. "Yes?"

"How do I do it?"

"Do what?"

"Try it. This attitude of yours. What do I do?"

The question puzzled her. After all, she'd never known anyone who didn't already have The Attitude.

"Well, I'm not really sure," she said, scratching her head. "Let me think." She lifted off his shoulder and floated back and forth in front of his face, a faery's equivalent, he supposed, of pacing. She stopped in midair, by his cheek and exclaimed "I know!" He waited for the explanation. "Just say the word you need!"

"What?"

"When you feel bad, just say the word you need. Like now. Try it right now!"

Allan squirmed. "I don't think–"

"Which word do you need right now? Hope, Possibility or Growth? Which one, Allan?"

He considered what she was asking. He thought about Catherine and how intensely he wanted her. He saw her with *him*, laughing, kissing, looking so content. A sick feeling clawed in the pit of his stomach. Ridiculous, he thought bitterly. What good could a single word do. This silly exercise is a waste of time.

"No, it's not!" Faery burst out. "Words have magic! Like flowers!"

Allan looked at her doubtfully. "Like flowers?"

"Yes!" She hovered over to a shock of vibrant yellow daffodils. "Words are alive! They vibrate! They have power!"

He studied the daffodils carefully, their graceful vibrant green stems and delicate trumpet-like flowers blazing with an orange core. He tried to think of Catherine. Instead, he flashed to the morning his mother died, how he had stood stiff, immobile, in the middle of their sunny kitchen, staring at a glass vase of wilted flowers. That same nauseating feeling gripping his insides. He felt small, weak, powerless, spiraling down and down, into an endless void.

"Pick a word," Faery encouraged.

He found himself thinking *hope*. It felt strange, like a foreign word. He thought it again, gently. Hope. He noticed a kind of fluttering in the center of his body. He said the word silently one more time: hope. This time he let out a deep sigh.

"See, it's working!" she exclaimed.

Hope. He thought it again and something lightened up inside him. He looked at Faery, blinking back tears. "Hope," he sighed. This time it made him smile.

20

"Ultimately, that is the definition of bravery:
not being afraid of yourself."
—Chogyum Trungpa

It took all his courage to go back to the cabin. From the top of the rise, he saw her sitting on the porch steps. Alone. At least he would be able to be with her, without *him.*

Catherine stood up to greet him, straightening the apron she wore over a long pale green dress. At that moment, she looked particularly innocent to him. His heart ached.

"Allan," she said, as he stopped a few feet in front of her. "I'm so sorry. I should have told you."

He shrugged. "You had no obligation."

"Oh, but I did." She stepped closer to take his hand. Her touch was electrifying. "I care about you, Allan. I never wanted to hurt you."

Looking into her eyes, warm and full of honesty, he couldn't bear the rising pain. He looked away. "Let's not talk about it. Okay?" He tried to take his hand back, but she held tighter.

"No," she answered firmly. "It's not okay."

He swallowed hard. "Catherine, there's really no point."

"Yes, there is." She led him to the porch steps to sit down beside her. Reluctantly, he obeyed. "Truth is always the point." She let his hand go and he stood up, trying to put more distance between them. "You have to tell me," she said softly, "how you feel."

A knot of terrible grief welled up in his chest. He held his breath, forcing it back down. He hated doing this. He hated it with a passion.

"Tell me," she said. "Please."

Unable to speak, all he could do was drink her in, like the last sip of nectar to a dying man. Her ruby hair was pulled loosely back, tied with a velvet ribbon, a blush of pink coloring her lips and cheeks. What could he possibly say? How wildly he loved her, how he would do anything, absolutely anything to have her. And how betrayed he felt, by her and by him, by Darkside, by the entire quest. He did not voice any of it. Instead, he climbed the steps. At the top of the porch, with his back turned to her, he declared, "There's no point,

Catherine." He headed into the house.

"Allan," she called. "Wait." He hesitated before closing the door behind him. "Can I ask you to do something for me?" His jaw stiffened as he watched her come up the

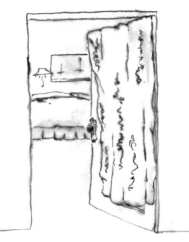

porch steps. "Please,' she begged. He nodded, knowing she was fully aware that he could never refuse her. "I want you to meet him." He looked at her in disbelief. "He's in my bedroom."

"Are you serious?"

She lowered her head. "He's ill, Allan. Dying."

He reeled. "What do you mean?"

"There's nothing anyone can do." She reached out to grab the porch railing, as if she needed support. "He doesn't have much time left. Please. Go inside and see him."

His hand slipped, like a dead weight, from the brass doorknob. Her request was insane. How could she expect him—how could she even think he would. She was watching him with such expectation, as if her request were the only thing in the world that mattered. He sighed and agreed.

She took his hand, leading him into the living room. The bedroom door was ajar, but he couldn't see inside.

"Go on," she urged gently. He glanced at her, then back at the door, frightened. "Remember one thing," she said as she tossed a small log into the fireplace. "Until you embrace your whole self, you can never be at peace." He didn't know what she meant. And at the moment, he didn't really care.

21

"And throughout all eternity
I forgive you, you forgive me."
—William Blake

THE MAN ON THE BED was breathing quietly, eyes closed. Allan stood in the doorway, afraid to go any further. He turned around to see if Catherine was watching. She sat down on the couch, pulling the woolen blanket around her shoulders, and nodded reassuringly. He steeled himself and walked inside. There was a chair beside the bed. Tentatively, he sat.

He didn't know what to think or what to do. It was strange to be sitting beside a dying man he didn't know. A man, in fact, whom he hated, who made his insides twist in painful knots.

Pale eyelids fluttered open and the man smiled.

"Thank you for coming," he said. Allan stared back

at him. He looked different than Allan remembered. He seemed much older, maybe twice Catherine's age. "It's hard for people," the man continued. "They feel uncomfortable." He winced, fighting a surge of pain. "We weren't raised to sit with death," he said. "It takes an open heart."

Allan couldn't speak. The man seemed so kind. How could that be possible, knowing the antagonism Allan felt. "Catherine," he finally said. "She asked me to come."

The man smiled. "She's wise beyond her years. Take care of her, will you?"

His words shocked Allan. This man whom he would have shot dead only hours before was now offering him the woman he loved. "Why are you treating me this way? I don't understand."

The man sighed, perplexed, then asked with great sincerity, "Is there another way to treat a human being?"

The question caught Allan off guard. "I guess not. But you're a better man than me."

He felt a growing impulse to relax, realizing that in spite of himself he actually liked the man. Quietly, the bedroom door closed. Catherine must have wanted them to have more privacy.

Looking down at the weakened figure, something odd began to happen. The man began to change, morph, his features slowly fading as a faint, silver haze washed over the face, gradually enveloping everything. Then a different face came back into view. The face of Allan's mother.

Paralyzed, he tried to make sense of what he was seeing. It couldn't be! His mother died almost four decades ago. But there she was, lying right in front of him, exactly as he remembered the day she died. Thin and weak, her long auburn hair, streaked with gray, spread out against the white cotton pillow. Her skin, almost translucent, made her green eyes shine even brighter. Despite her terrible illness, he thought she was still beautiful.

"Allan," she whispered. Startled by the sound of her voice, he looked frantically around the room. What was happening? How was this possible? "Listen to me." He leaned closer, searching her face, but she looked right through him. "Your father, Allan," she said, "he loves me. He loves me more than you can possibly know."

A piercing pain twisted inside him. He remembered those words. He remembered standing at her bedside, as a seven-year-old boy, holding her hand, listening to those very words. "You're too young now," she went on in a weak voice, "but someday, I promise, I swear to you on all the angels in heaven, someday you will know that depth of love. And then you'll understand."

He didn't move. He sat, transfixed, watching and listening. She had spoken those very words to him as a child. And he remembered now how hard it was for him to hear them. He had pleaded with her not to die, refusing to let in what she was saying. She was right, of course. He was much too young then to understand those things. And much too wounded by the immensity of his loss.

His soul ached. He wanted to speak, to reach out and touch her. Her face began to change, features blurring, again morphing. He sat, hypnotized by the haunting events, so out of his control. Another face emerged, slightly larger, rounder, much older. It was his father.

Raw, painful memories flashed in quick succession. A small boy sobbing in a corner, clutching a photograph of a woman with green eyes. A father cursing a young boy hunched over a shattered glass of milk. The harsh white cell of a hospital room. A dying anguished old man.

"Why did you treat me that way?" Allan seethed, "all those years. Why?"

"The day she died," his father whispered, as if in mid-sentence to someone else, "I thought that would be the worst moment of my life." He hesitated. "I was wrong." Allan tensed, overwhelmed with emotion. He knew he didn't belong here. He felt like a voyeur, like someone hiding behind a confessional curtain. His father never looked up or stopped talking. "Day after day, night after night, I couldn't bear the emptiness. It was as if my heart had been ripped from my chest." He coughed weakly, sucking in a breath. Allan could see how truly sick he was. "I knew I had to go on," he whispered fiercely. "To care for my son, *our* son. The only part of her I had left. But every day when I looked at him," he began to weep, "I only saw *her*, *her* face, *her* eyes, *her* life. I couldn't bear it. Do you hear me? God forgive me, I couldn't bear *him*."

Allan clawed the arms of the chair, grief threatening to choke him. The old man went on. "We grew up in a terrible silence. A silence no young child deserves. I had no way of filling it. No way at all." Immobilized, Allan tried desperately not to cry out, tears streaming down his cheeks, immersed in a depth of sadness he had never known. "I loved him," his father pleaded, "Dear Lord, I loved him more than myself. Forgive me. Forgive me for what I've done."

The features began to blur again. Allan held his breath, afraid of what would come next. Through the same haze a new face slowly faded into view, a man not much older than himself. Allan went completely limp realizing the face he stared down at was his own. In the bed lay the dying figure of Allan Quinn Fitzpatrick.

With every ounce of strength, he tried to get up. To run. But a powerful energy held him prisoner.

"I've lived poorly," his weakened counterpart confessed. "The things in life that really matter—family, friends, love—I didn't cultivate. Too much anger. Too much self-hatred." The dying man could not stop an onslaught of tears. "I failed everyone," he cried desperately. "I'm so ashamed." Lifting a feeble hand, he begged, "Forgive me. Please...forgive me."

Time stopped. A bright stillness washed the room. With a tenderness Allan never thought possible, he accepted the hand of his dying self. Looking deeply into the pained blue eyes, he said, "I do forgive you. I forgive you for everything."

His mirror-self let go a peaceful sigh. "Thank you," he whispered, closing his eyes for the last time.

"I forgive you," Allan murmured again. "I do." He held the hand for a long time, a hand so familiar, still warm with a life that once was. Gently he folded the arms across the chest. Standing up, a languid peace settled around him, like the dusting of a first snow. He glanced in the mirror on the bureau. His blue eyes were softer now. Glistening with something different, something he had never seen before. "Compassion," a sweet voice offered. He turned to see Faery hovering beside his cheek. She reached out her tiny hand and let her fingers brush his skin.

"Compassion," she sang again, shimmering. "The Second Sacred Branch."

He thought of the book. And he knew the pages would be filled again. A new world of wisdom waiting for him, a world he was hungry for. He walked back into the living room. Catherine was sitting quietly on the couch. "He's gone," she said with a painful knowing. Allan touched her shoulder. He accepted now the extraordinary visions that were a natural part of Darkside.

"He died peacefully."

She smiled sadly. "Thank you, Allan."

That night, he stayed up late reading the book and writing in his journal. The first set of pages from Praise had disappeared. They were now filled anew with the Second Sacred Branch: "Compassion is the greatest law of the forest," the book said, "because it is the act of *including*."

The explanation surprised him. "Much of humanity has forgotten this fundamental law. The forgetting has caused great wars and inflicted terrible pain throughout the centuries—pain born from a different law, an unnatural one, the law of Hate, the act of *excluding*."

Allan contemplated the words. "Compassion," the book emphasized, "is simply the willingness to include all things."

It was as if a light went on inside him, a flood of insight. He hurried to his journal and began writing feverishly. He wrote about the life-long rage he felt toward his father, and the terrible shame hiding beneath; the shame of a little boy grown into a man who had never been the right kind of son. He realized how much he had buried those pieces of himself, refused to include them, because they didn't match his ideas, his image, his impossible expectations. He realized how much of his childhood pain he had turned away from and discarded.

He went back to the book. "The forest floor accepts all things that fall upon it. Dead and broken branches, leaves and plants diseased, the rotting carcass of the fox, the smooth, clean bones of the once mighty bear. These ill and death-filled things nurture the forest. They are welcomed wholeheartedly back into the cycle of life. Nothing, absolutely nothing is excluded from the forest floor."

More realizations swept through him, illuminating secrets he'd kept veiled and hidden in the dark. Passionately, he continued writing. The tenderness he felt for the trees and flowers in Central Park and how he refused to share that with a single soul. He now saw the tragedy of that decision and how excluding that part of himself only caused great suffering. When he began to add up all the pieces of himself he had rejected over the years of his life, there was very little of Allan left. Even his jealousy toward Catherine's lover. When he looked at the core of that pain, he could see once again that he was rejecting, *excluding* from *his* forest floor, that potent human emotion.

"Until you embrace your own whole self," Catherine had told him, "you can never be at peace." Now he understood what she meant. He let out a sigh, then turned back to the book. A sentence jumped out at him.

"The truest form of love," it said, "is Compassion—the willingness to include all things."

When he finally fell asleep, it was just as the sun rose over faraway mountains, just as the distant eagle folded its wings from the long flight home. For the first time in his life, he slept with a smile on his face. Because for the first time in his life he was sleeping with all of himself.

22

"What we choose to fight is so tiny!
What fights with us is so great!
If only we could let ourselves be dominated
as things do by some immense storm,
we would grow strong too and not need names."
—Rainer Maria Rilke

STANDING WITH HIS BACK against a massive stone wall, he stares terror-stricken at the approaching nightmare. Swirling pillars of light, reaching up to the sky, march toward him, bright soldiers of death. Every advance brings the deafening crack of thunder and lightning.

Twisting around, he claws at the hard stone, trapped, nowhere to run, knowing that behind the wall awaits a shelter, a refuge that can protect him from this terrible thing. It is an impenetrable fortress, this wall, with no doors, no windows, no way to get inside. Stricken with fear, he crumples to the ground.

Three figures approach, shrouded in fog. The pillars of death advance closely behind them. The figures moved slowly, showing no fear of the looming danger.

The fog clears and he gasps, startled to see Catherine, Ethel Goodwoman, and a much larger Faery, the size of a young girl. They reach him, singing in unison, "Hello, Allan."

He doesn't understand their peaceful composure. "The pillars!" he cries, pointing in terror at the impending doom. They throw their heads back and laugh.

The three women kneel down before the colossal stone wall. They stay motionless, heads touching the ground, as if in reverent prayer.

The pillars of light advance relentlessly. He leaps up, gripped with a choking panic. "They're coming!" he screams. "For God's sakes, they're coming! Get up! Get up!"

Chanting softly, they do not seem to hear him. His attention is torn between their calm repose and the impending doom.

Gracefully rising together, they stand. Each faces the wall, placing their hands, palm down, on the hard stone. In horrified fascination, he watches as they begin to meld into the thick smooth surface. First a hand disappears, then an elbow, an arm, a shoulder. Bodies vanishing into stone. Faery and Ethel Goodwoman beam brightly at him, then pull themselves through. Only Catherine partially remains.

"Don't leave me!" he cries out. "Please, Catherine, don't leave me!" Her body slowly begins merging into the wall. "Come back, Catherine, please!" Sobbing like a child, he twists around to see the monstrous swirling light almost upon him. Catherine's smiling face is the last thing he sees, then she vanishes, leaving him helpless before the cold, impenetrable wall. "How did you do that?" he pleads, beating bloodied fists against stone. "How did you do that?!"

He hears a woman's voice respond. He cannot tell if it is Catherine or Ethel or Faery. Yet the words are crystal clear. "Surrender, Allan," she says. "Surrender."

Early morning. An unearthly howl. The sound of shattering glass forced him awake. Bolting upright in bed, he looked out the window. Rain and darkness blanketed the woods. Trees and branches groaned. He dressed quickly and hurried into the living room. The cabin was empty.

Suddenly, the front door burst open. Catherine stood there, in the downpour, hair soaked and matted.

"The storm, Allan! You must go! Now!" She swept past him, into her bedroom, carrying out a small cloth bundle. "Now!" she commanded, rushing through the cabin toward the muddy path outside.

"Catherine!" he shouted. Another explosion of glass. The window by the front door. Shards scattered across the living room floor. An icy gust swept in, chilling him to the bone. "Wait! What's going on?!" She spun around, wind whipping her clothes and hair. "What's happening? What is this?" he pleaded. She looked at him, eyes flashing through the torrential rain, and smiled. Then turned and ran away.

Confused, panicked, he raced to his room, grabbed the book, his journal, a jacket, and fled. The ferocious storm assaulted him, making it almost impossible to see where he was headed. Shoving the books under his jacket, he took off to catch up to her. Leaves and twigs spiraled wildly in the air like mini tornadoes; battered branches creaked and moaned. Blindly, he stumbled along the path, hoping she was just ahead. In the distance, a shriek. Human or animal?

"Catherine!" he screamed. He ran as fast as he could, soaked to the skin, the tempest bearing down on him. The sky grew darker, trees bending, twisting, pummeled by the furious squall. "Catherine?!" he shouted again, fighting despair. "Where are you?"

Another high-pitched shriek. He ran even faster. A sinister bolt of white light speared a nearby tree, a blackthorn, toppling the tall prickly shrub right in front of him. Unable to stop his momentum, he tumbled over it, caught in the branches, thorns slashing his legs, book and journal scattering in different directions.

Lying on the muddy earth, heaving and panting, legs bloodied, he remembered the dream. Fingernails clawing stone. Catherine slipping away. He had to find her, save her. Crawling to the journal, he shoved it back under his jacket, and tried to stand. An agonizing pain shot through his ankle, and he collapsed. The book, a few feet away, lay open beside a huge boulder. The pages were blank. The Second Sacred Branch. The words already gone.

Then he heard her voice behind him. "Allan."

Desperately, he twisted around, scanning the shadowy forest. She was nowhere in sight. "Where are you, Catherine?" he cried out. "Where are you?"

"The time has come," she called, her voice muffled by the din of the storm. "To meet... "

Lightning and thunder roared across the angry sky. He could no longer hear her. "Catherine! What? To meet what?"

High above, black clouds churned and roiled like savage seas. Electric streaks pierced the eerie night. "...to meet your greatest fear."

A paralyzing dread began to take hold. Achingly familiar. "Don't go!" he screamed. "Please!" Memories, like tidal waves. The last day with his mother. The last hour. Clinging, clutching, being dragged away. Sobbing, alone in his room. The next morning, grief so crushing it threatened to decimate him.

Ankle throbbing, tamping down the devastating feelings, he dragged himself to the book. He needed to save the book. As he gathered the sacred tome under his jacket, he spotted a small opening in the boulder, like the entrance to a cave. Desperately wanting to rest, to get his bearings, just for a moment, he crawled inside—the shelter barely large enough to hold him. Slumped against the cold stone, he willed himself to take slow measured breaths. The storm would abate. Soon. It had to. Then he would find Catherine. Then he would be with her. Then everything would be alright.

The vicious storm did not cease, blotting out the sun, leaving forest creatures quaking in secret hiding places. Huddled against the cave's smooth wall, he noticed, in the corner, a small bird shivering in the darkness. His distress momentarily retreated as he inched closer to get a better look.

She was a common finch, brown with wisps of white, newly out of the nest. A pale delicate beak peeked out from a soft mound of soaked, ruffled feathers. And her eyes, perfect round dots, glimmered in the cave's flickering shadow. Despite the violent storm, he wondered how something this fragile and vulnerable could be so beautiful.

Those thoughts faded as the demon winds raged on, mercilessly, as if trying to obliterate everything in their path. Hours melted into days, days into nights. He barely moved, growing weaker and weaker. Finally, unable to sit upright, he crumpled to the ground, knowing he'd never make it out of the forest alive. That he would never see Catherine again.

With his last bit of strength, he cried to the womb-like darkness, "What should I do?" Like he did the night his mother died. "Please, someone tell me, what should I do?"

Fading out of consciousness, he heard a reply.

Surrender, Allan. Surrender.

And after a lifetime of fighting, after a lifetime of resisting, after a lifetime of running, he finally did.

23

"What makes you vulnerable, makes you beautiful."
—Brené Brown

As HE LAY ON THE MOIST EARTH in a state of being few ever reach, words flowed. This time not on soft bark paper bound within the primordial book. One by one the teachings unfolded within him: "The Third Sacred Branch of the Ancient Realm is known only as Surrender. To kneel in reverence before that which cannot be controlled. To humbly accept what stands before you."

In this otherworldly realm, a place beyond dreaming, beyond all notions understood by the human mind, the wisdom continued: "There is no thing or being in Nature that is not in a complete and constant state of Surrender. For Surrender is a state of true vulnerability. And vulnerability is the essence of all that is beautiful on earth."

Had he been awake, in a state of ordinary awareness, he would have tried to make sense of those words. Because vulnerability, to him and to many others, meant very different things. Weak things, useless things. Things without power or strength. He would have asked, how are beauty and vulnerability related to this thing called Surrender?

In the place he rested now, where the veil between mind and spirit is lifted, where the heart is pure, the place all men and women dream about in dreams they cannot remember, the words flowed on: "All of Nature is vulnerable. A towering tree can be felled by a sharp blade, a howling wind, the fury of fire. A tree cannot save

Surrender

To Humbly
Accept
What Stands
Before You

itself. A wildflower cannot flee. It is this very act, this pure state of Surrender, this pose of absolute vulnerability that imbues each of them with glory. This is the paradox and the secret of all things beautiful on earth."

If he were awake reading these words, turning the pages beneath the soft afternoon light, he might have stopped to ponder this teaching. To think about the essence of its meaning. He might have recalled the miraculous peapod he once loved, that brought him so much comfort. He might have understood how its fragile strength and need for sun and rain were intimately connected to its tender beauty. He might have realized the paradox of Surrender.

"All things beautiful are vulnerable," the words sang to him in melodies that mortal beings could only hope to hear. "A newly blossomed tulip, a cooing infant, a streak of sunset across the sea—these expressions of beauty can, in any moment, be wiped away. The most beautiful moments on earth are the most vulnerable ones. Think on this."

In the place he rested now, this ancient wisdom took hold. The veils lifted and he relived those memories he spent a lifetime running from. The last days with his mother, when her face shone with a beauty he had never seen before; when the room she lay dying in filled with the light of a Divine presence.

In this liminal space, he relived, with immense sadness, the last moments of his father, remembering what he tried all his life to forget. That something extraordinary happened that day. Something more than dying. That the moment his father let go the final breath, that same Divine light filled the room; the same luminous peace settled softly on his father's anguished face. In those precious last moments, he vividly remembered how his father shone with the same radiant beauty he beheld on the face of his mother. He witnessed his father—a man who fought hard to deny an aching love for wife and son—lay down his arms and, at long last, surrender.

It was daybreak when Allan stirred from this deep ethereal slumber. The morning sun glittered. The forest, though rattled and shaken, remained. Creatures winged and legged, sleek and scaled, stones adorned in moss, ferns and flowers, clouds and rivers—all sentient things reborn.

He crawled out of the cave, into the sunlight, tears streaming. He was crying not because the storm had ended, not because he had survived. He was crying because he remembered. Each and every word. They lived inside him now as if each letter had been carved upon the thin membrane of his heart.

On his knees, he wept. For years lost, for years wasted, for words never spoken, for lonely boys abandoned by their Selves. He wept for women he never loved, for those who never loved him, and for the tenderness he never allowed himself to feel. He wept for his mother and father and the gifts they gave him.

Cleansed, he drank in the surrounding forest. Pearl-sized dew drops clung hopefully to the tips of translucent leaves. Newborn ferns, still curled from sleep, glittered with the moistness of a new dawn. Everything around him shimmered with a vulnerability that was almost too beautiful to bear.

Kneeling, he bowed, his forehead touching the moist brown soil. A sense of holiness swept over him, flooding his being, deepening the essence of all he had learned. *To Kneel in Reverence Before That Which Cannot Be Controlled. To Humbly Accept That Which Stands Before You.* In gratitude, he touched his lips to the earth. And he understood, with a transcendent knowing, he had completed the Quest.

Part Four

Revelation

"It is no strange fate
You read these words.
We have been waiting for you.
You who hold these pages in your hands.
The time has come.
Do not be afraid.
The Ancient Realms speak to you.
Remember, please remember."

—The Ancient Book of Fae

24

"The temple bell stops –
but the sound keeps coming out of the flowers."
—Basho

Allan walked for a long time, his ankle and leg fully healed, trusting the path would lead him out of the forest. The ancient book was safe under his arm, a precious talisman, a holy memory of all he had experienced. He knew the pages would be blank. Everything he needed was written in his journal. Woven in his very being.

Though he hadn't eaten in days, he wasn't hungry or thirsty. His body felt strong and alive. There was no point going back for Catherine. Real or illusory, she and Darkside were gone. He would miss them terribly.

Stopping by a wide stream, he slipped off his shoes and bathed his tired feet. The water felt refreshingly cool. He cupped a handful and drank.

The water's surface, mirror like, reflected a floating image. The face of a man who had profoundly changed, a face graced with gentleness and beauty.

He wrote with abandon in his journal, pouring out pages and pages of feelings. He wrote about eternal teachings and miraculous experiences and the transformative journey into himself. He set the leather notebook down and picked up the old, fraying book made of bark and leaves and sap. Lovingly he touched the cover, hoping the ancient treasure would survive the long trip back to New York. He would preserve it, in glass, like a museum display, as a perpetual reminder of the truth.

On impulse he opened the book to the first page, the fragile sheet crumbling around the edges. He focused on the parchment, trying to remember how it looked covered with the bold jade script he'd grown to love. He thought again of Catherine, his *anam cara*, and how much he still loved her, wondering who she really was and if she would go back to a life he could never hope to understand. For a brief moment, he wished he could stay in Darkside forever, wander the woods, write the book that had been eluding him all these years, and at night sleep beside the woman with fire hair. He ached because he knew how truly impossible that would be.

He remembered Faery and The Attitude. What word did he need now? Possibility. When he looked back down at the page, a sentence gradually seeped through. "Darkside is always closer than you think." He smiled. Then the words vanished.

Collecting the books, he continued on the winding path. Sadness mixed with quiet anticipation, he was aware the forest would soon end, thrusting him back into the Irish countryside back onto a plane heading home, back to the noisy, bustling world he'd left behind.

Ahead of him, a shaft of light showered the path. Quickening his pace, he stepped into the shimmering area where light met earth. Looking up, he saw another bright column flooding a new trail that veered to the right. Curious, he stopped. As far as the eye could see, a vision of endless paths illuminated by pure white light, like branches of a luminescent tree.

Instinctively he opened the book. Two new sentences in fresh ink. "Walk a thousand misty roads and your head will never find it. Walk with your heart and there it shall forever be."

Perplexed, he thought the Quest had ended. The Sacred Branches lived within him now. Praise. Compassion. Surrender. Hadn't he learned all that Darkside meant to teach him? Was there something more? Following the main path, he passed what looked like hundreds of alternate trails bathed in surreal radiance.

He continued walking, noticing, much to his dismay, his strength draining. Growing wearier with each step, he pushed on, something propelling him to keep going. Finally, unable to continue, he laid down on the path. Despite the exhaustion, he trusted what was happening, wondering where this never-ending journey was taking him now. Looking up at the sky, he listened to the forest: trees rustling, the whistling wind, the chorus of birds and buzzing insects. Soon an unfamiliar sound emerged. A faint melody, otherworldly, like voices, though he couldn't recognize any words. The sound grew louder and louder, then the ground began trembling. He struggled to stand, turning in the direction of the ethereal music, and gasped. A radiant pillar of brilliant emerald light soared far beyond the treetops. And spinning round the luminous column were thousands of extraordinary creatures, an endless procession of beings in every shape, size and color—green-skinned, chestnut brown, pale yellow, and black as midnight, others, pearly white as the moon. Some were tiny, the length of fingers, others not taller than a child. Some had hideous wrinkled profiles, bodies gnarled and knotted, others were soft and innocent, draped in glittering dew.

Mesmerized, Allan watched as they spun around and around the emerald pillar, melodious sounds emanating more beautiful than any he had ever heard. They didn't seem to notice him. Or care. They whirled, like creatures on a mythical carousel, around this spellbinding tower of light.

As the tones softened, a new sound emerged. A voice, one that he recognized immediately: Faery! Within the unending stream of mystical creatures, he could hear her but not see her. Faery's voice resonated as the sublime music faded to a quiet hum.

"The time has come, Allan," she declared with great power, "to see us as we truly are." As she spoke, he focused more clearly on the remarkable beings circling the pillar. "Throughout the ages," Faery began, "humankind has seen us with countless different faces." He recognized many of the creatures, remembering them from childhood picture books. Olive-skinned elves with pointed ears wearing silvery slippers that curled at the toes; child-sized leprechauns donning tall black hats, carrying pots brimming with gold; and delicate sprites and fairies wearing long, sheer gossamer gowns. "Whatever humankind believed about the world around them," Faery went on in her disembodied voice, "that was how we were seen. If wind and thunder frightened them, we were dark and hideous. If traveling through the woods brought them terror, we were night servants who stole their children." Many of the faces were fearsome. Gnomes dancing by whose features seemed carved from twisted roots and stone. Ghostly figures with wispy hair and wild eyes glowing like embers. "Whatever humankind believed about their world, that was the mask we were made to wear. If they believed us to be like themselves, civilized and full of grace, then we were winged, as angels, playing flutes and harps."

Awestruck, Allan watched the pageant of numinous beings. As they spun past him, he noticed how some were dressed in traditional clothing: silk kimonos dyed red and yellow, skirts woven of grass and palm fronds, fur-skinned parkas and leather boots, necklaces strung with bleached bones and feathers, as if they were representing every nation in the world. A fantastic multicultural procession of supernatural citizens.

"From every corner of this earth," Faery continued, "they named us different things. Some called us fallen angels, others the spirits of the dead. In the West they named us fairy, elf, gnome, forest nymph, elementals and brownies, knockers, cobolds, water babies and earth-manikins. In the East they claimed us as devas, jinn, and demi-gods, leshys and domovays. In the South they christened us yumboes and menehune, and in the North, tomtes and nisses.

"But none of these names and none of these masks has ever been the truth." She paused as the circle of beings began spinning faster. "Until this moment, humankind has never been ready. The time has come to see us as we truly are."

Faster and faster the creatures whirled, spiraling at an unimaginable speed, blurring, merging, the mystical humming infusing every atom in the air until they melded into a vast ring of rainbow light, pulsing hypnotically. "We are the Children of Fae," she said, her voice growing deeper, beyond recognition. "The benevolent guardians of Earth who dwell within Her Hidden Kingdom. We are Her protectors, Her expressions, Her own Divine Beings of Praise."

Allan stood motionless, enthralled, reverberating within cosmic sounds and tones. The voice, no longer Faery's, genderless and omnipresent, spoke again in a melodic rhythm.

"We are the wind upon your face,
We are the song of birds at dawn,
We are the sparkling virgin glacier,
We are the velvet rose newborn.
We are the slender blade of grass,
We are the insects who must thrive,
See us in everything on earth,
See us in all things alive."

He felt his body expanding, filling up with something primordial, indescribable, intensifying with the promise to overflow. And the voice sang on:

"It is not the golden shaft of wheat
that fills your body's hungry yearning.
It is not the coo of the mourning dove

that soothes your heart's most painful burning.
The song you hear when the sparrow sings
is Our True Song within her sound.
And the color seen that the rainbow brings
is from Our Light spreading all around.
Our Presence dwells within all alive,
It is Us you feel in all things that thrive."

Tossing his head back in ecstasy, he blissfully surrendered to the potent, lyrical words, the sacred sounds emanating from the spheres of light, the choral praise of a hundred thousand Divine beings.

From deep within him began a rumbling. Harmonious, symphonic sounds seeping into every cell, every fiber of his being, throbbing, swelling to a point he could no longer contain. Like a volcano, melodies erupted, shooting out from every pore of his body. Exquisite sound! His sound! His voice! Out it poured, like orchestral stardust, through fingers and toes, lifting him higher and higher, through belly and chest, through every strand of hair on his head. His whole body singing!

Somewhere in the far reaches of his mind, he watched a different scene. He saw Catherine, dressed in white, hair glowing like embers. "Tell me, Allan," she asked. "What is it like to sing to the forest?" Allan's being sang of ecstatic union with everything.

She bowed her head. "That's prayer," she offered. "True prayer is the purest song." Slowly, the vision faded. Settling back into his body, the pulsing rainbow light dimmed. Looking down at his feet, he realized he had never moved at all.

"This is who we are," the voice declared again. "The world has never been ready until now."

In a flash, the spheres of light imploded, vanishing completely, leaving him standing alone, staring up at the soaring emerald pillar.

He felt a tremor beneath his feet. Every tree and branch and leaf shuddered. The enormous pillar began changing color. Green muted into yellow, yellow spilled into orange, orange burned to red, then flowed into violet, warming to a rich glowing amber. The ground quaked. An explosion of blinding white light. His hands flew up, covering his face as he fell to his knees.

"The time has come," the voice commanded, "To enter the Garden of the Heart!"

25

"There is infinite space in your garden;
all men, all women are welcome here;
all they need do is enter."
—The Odes of Solomon

WHERE THE PILLER OF LIGHT once stood, a celestial tree now grew, grander and more magnificent than any tree on earth. Its bark was iridescent silver, as supple as skin. Three colossal branches covered in folds and creases like massive arms grew out of the mammoth trunk. The branches themselves touched the clouds and were almost bare except for a scattering of shimmering greenish-gold leaves. From the base of the holy tree crawled three gigantic roots, knotted and gnarled like mythical serpents. Around the tree blossomed infinite flowers—flowers from every garden and forest and meadow and mountain on earth, flowers in every bright and vibrant color, in every subtle shade, in every fragile texture, in every strong and sturdy way. A divine, dazzling masterpiece of terrestrial beauty. And cradled deep within the center of the tree's immense body, a cavernous womb sheltered an enormous living, beating heart.

Head tilted back, drinking in this rapturous vision, Allan's gaze soared upward, tracing the tree's endless trunk. Spellbound, his inner sight opened, revealing the molten red life-force. The beating of this titanic heart, a steady rhythm, like pounding surf, like eternal drums, surged through him. He fell to his knees, in reverence, before this hallowed sight.

He felt no fear, knowing this was a blessed place, a sanctuary. He had entered the sacred home where all things take root, where all things begin, where all things grow eternally. He had entered the Garden of the Heart.

Contemplating this boundless sentient vision, the naked branches stretching to the heavens, he was overcome with an inexplicable sense of loss. He remained kneeling, trying to understand this palpable sorrow. Allowing his shoulders and head to drop, he bowed fully, touching the earth. He stayed in this prayerful pose for a long time, feeling the resounding heartbeat. Slowly the cadenced sound morphed into a fiercely benevolent voice.

"We have been waiting for You. You who bow before

us. You who have held the pages in your hands. The time has come. Do not be afraid. You are the Chosen One." His whole body trembled. "You who kneel before us now, bowed humbly in reverence.

"You who have remembered the ancient secrets, the living branches of Truths that dwell within this beating heart and within the heart of all Children of Fae. The time has come to listen to the final bidding." He soaked in each word vibrating through his very core.

"Since time immemorial this garden flourished as a living testament to all that is sacred and good in the world. The branches of the tree were filled. With every fallen leaf, more grew in its place. The heart of the world remained strong. The tree thrived.

"Then came a time when, one by one, leaves dropped to the ground and nothing more flourished. It was the will of humanity, that with each passing century, the Sacred Branches of Truth grew bare within their hearts. The Praising ceased, Compassion scattered in the winds of hatred, the holiness of Surrender long forgotten. The garden grew weaker and weaker. And now, these three branches, with few leaves remaining, stretch unadorned, existing only because of those who have refused to abandon the Quest."

Overcome with emotion, Allan placed a hand on his

chest as the voice continued. "For this tree to flourish again, every man and woman on the face of the earth must remember what they have forgotten. Every human being must carry back into their life the sacred song of Praise, Compassion, and Surrender. For each who reclaims these precious branches, who humbly acknowledges the Divine purpose that is their birthright, who willingly accepts the Quest, these branches and this tree shall bloom once more."

High above his head, on all three branches, glimmering buds of emerald and jade emerged. Bursting, blossoming, shimmering across all three massive boughs, into full-fledged shining leaves, flecked with gold. The voice spoke again: "For each and every man and woman who carries these Sacred Branches back into their heart, seventeen new leaves shall grow. And with each rising

sun, seventeen more. Yours have been added. In humble gratitude, they bow before You."

A warm breeze swept through the forest. Allan watched as the glistening new leaves shivered gently in the soft wind, bending in his direction.

"RISE!" the voice boomed. Reverently, Allan rose to his feet. "Go now, back to the place you call home and teach all whom you meet these blessed things. Many will listen. Many will turn away. Be not afraid. Let your heart speak what you know every day for the rest of your life."

He bowed his head in understanding. He gratefully accepted the benediction and had no confusion or resistance about the enormity of the task.

"Without these branches filled," the voice continued, "without new leaves growing, this tree cannot flourish. This garden cannot grow. The heart of this world cannot thrive.

"Go now," the voice commanded. "And let these branches one day soon bask in the glory that is their Divine destiny."

He looked up one last time at the sacred vision before him. Collecting his books, he turned around and continued down the path. In a brilliant flash of light, the tree was gone, hidden once more within its protective emerald pillar, enveloped forever by the mystical beings he once knew as Faery. Waves of sadness washed over him. He wanted to look back, but didn't, comforted by the sound of an immortal beating heart merging with his own.

When he reached the edge of the forest and saw the familiar stone cottage in the distance, he walked slowly, savoring every step.

Mrs. O'Sullivan was pruning her rose bush when she spotted him. She said nothing because he didn't notice her. He was intently praising the tall sunflower plant nearby. She set down her pruning shears, wiped her broad forehead with the worn cotton towel she had used for years, and sat down on the old wooden stool. Nodding, she watched him as she patted a small round gold pin hidden beneath her apron. "He's seen," she whispered to her garden, eyes gleaming. "He's *seen*."

26

"Love is the only gold."
—Alfred Lord Tennyson

THEY ALL STOOD OUTSIDE the cottage, waiting for the taxi to arrive.

"We're so glad we met you," Edna O'Sullivan said. She stepped forward and shyly kissed Allan on the cheek.

"Please...come back," her husband added.

Allan reached out to shake his hand. In an unexpected outburst of emotion, Patrick O'Sullivan pulled him to his chest, and they hugged.

"I'm sorry about the truck," Allan said. "As soon as I get back to New York, I'll wire you the money."

"No need a 'tall," Edna O'Sullivan piped in. She winked, nodding toward the side of the house. There, partially hidden under tall grasses, glistening in the morning sun, sat the vintage pick up, sporting only a few minor dents in the front end. "Nothing that my Patrick can't fix."

Allan laughed, knowing there was no logical explanation. When the taxicab pulled into the gravel driveway and honked, he hugged Edna one last time. The taxi's dark tinted windows were rolled up, obscuring the driver.

"You're sure, now, you don't want your suitcase?" Mrs. O'Sullivan asked, for yet the fifth time. "American clothes are expensive."

"Keep them," he said. "I need a new wardrobe." He smiled warmly. "To go with a new life." He looked fondly at the O'Sullivans, aware he would probably never see them again. "Take care, both of you." Edna and Patrick stood arm in arm, as the taxi drove off.

"Dublin Airport," Allan said, settling comfortably into the back seat.

"In a hurry, are you now, to get back to the big city?" It was a woman's voice, a very familiar one.

He nearly leapt out of his seat when he saw Ethel Goodwoman at the wheel. "How did you—"

"When will you stop asking those silly questions?" she said, whisking off the black woolen fisherman's cap, fluffing her silver gray hair, and donning her green velvet hat. He grinned from ear to ear, delighted to see her again. "So," she said, glancing in the rear-view mirror, "are you ready for everything waiting back home?"

"I don't know," he sighed. "The world out there looks like a pretty scary place."

Ethel Goodwoman winked. "The world out there only *looks* real," she said. "Don't be fooled."

He laughed. "Well, then, I guess I'm ready."

"That's my boy," she chirped. "I knew I could count on you."

The conversation quieted as they rode in silence. So much had changed since he arrived. He felt transformed. How long had he been gone? Weeks? Months? He had no idea.

Reading his thoughts, she grinned. "You'll arrive in New York City on the first day of Spring."

"What? That's March 21st."

She shot him a bemused glance. "I'm well aware of that auspicious day."

"But how can that be?" he asked in disbelief. "I left on March 19th. I must have been gone for at least three weeks!"

She grinned. "Darkside is a funny sort of place. Things move slowly there...in a quick sort of way."

"I'll miss it," he confessed. "I'll miss everything."

"You won't have time," she argued happily. "There's much more for you to do."

They arrived at Dublin Airport much sooner than he wanted. It would have been fine had she taken a longer route, perhaps one that would have indefinitely delayed his return.

She parked beneath a particularly majestic oak tree, its glossy leaves brimming with hazel acorns, then joined him in the back seat. She was wearing pants, green velvet of course, and a matching green silk blouse.

"You've done well," she said in a more serious tone. Taking his hand in hers, she added, "We're all very proud, Allan. You're one of us now." Flooded with a child-like warmth, he smiled, appreciating her kindness.

"Mrs. Goodwoman," he began, a bit anxiously.

"Call me Ethel, dear. We're family now."

"Alright." He hesitated. "Ethel, I have to ask. I mean, I wondered about this since the beginning. Well, with all the green velvet you wear, and that unusual hat of yours..."

She tapped the top of the hat with great affection, squashing it down a bit. "Brilliant, isn't

it?" she said. "An old friend custom made it for me. Has a delightful millinery shop right here in Dublin."

He looked at her, feeling foolish. Could it be...after all that happened to him...would it be improbable to believe she could actually be—

"A leprechaun?" laughed Ethel Goodwoman. "I'm flattered, Allan. A fantastic society, really. Quick thinkers. Nimble, too. To be quite honest, though, they're a tad nitpicky for my taste and I've never been a fan of their cast iron pots. Besides, we have very different focuses. I offer a chance to find your *inner* gold."

He glanced down at the ancient book beside him, relieved it had held up this far, hoping it would make the journey intact. He needed one tangible keepsake to ward off any middle-of-the-night doubt. Besides, he wasn't taking much else back. Just his journal and the clothes he was wearing.

"At least I have this," he said proudly, lifting the book. It crumbled, falling apart in his hands, spraying bits of wood, leaves, and bark across the seat. "No!" he shouted. "Oh, no!"

She patted his hand. "Now, now. You've got the most important one." She gestured to the leather-bound journal on the seat beside him. "That's the only book that counts."

"But I wanted..." He swallowed his words, overcome with sadness.

"I know this is difficult for you, Allan," she said. "Giving up so many things. Catherine, Darkside, and now the book." She smiled compassionately. "Remember what Faery taught you. I think you need the G word now."

He hesitated. "Growth," he said softly. She went on.

"There will always be challenges. Stone walls to conquer, obstacles and disappointments we never expected. The secret," she added, "is to do what the trees do." He waited, expectantly. "When they encounter an obstacle in their path, they simply include it by growing around it. And never, for one moment, Allan, do they stop reaching for the sun."

He knew she was right. Growth. A knot of resistance tightened his stomach. He thought—and felt—the word again. Growth. His body relaxed, surrendering into acceptance. Ethel Goodwoman unfastened the small gold brooch on her lapel. With reverence, she pinned it to Allan's shirt, beneath his collar.

"You earned this. Wear it well."

He embraced her. She hugged him back as if he were her son. "What about you?" he asked. "This is your pin. I shouldn't take it."

She held up her hand to quiet him, then reached into a velvet carpetbag and pulled out a small wooden case. Carefully, she unlocked it with a silver key. Inside, pinned to the plush green cloth were dozens of the same round gold pin. Allan shook his head, smiling. "I have to admit I'm still a little disappointed that I'm not the only one." They laughed and hugged again.

Inside the terminal, check in went smoothly. In the whirlwind of the past few days, he hadn't booked a flight. After all he had been through on this Quest, he trusted there would be a seat waiting for him. He wasn't surprised to find only first class available. A fitting way to end a rather phenomenal journey.

Strolling outside to say his final good-byes, he saw Ethel Goodwoman leaning against the cab door, puffing a thin cigar. He chuckled. She looked like a New York cabbie. They waved fondly at each other. Something unusual glittered on the car's front end. A hood ornament? Inching closer, he burst into a wide grin. Perched on the hood, wings shimmering, was Faery, smiling, no, beaming at him, looking more beautiful and precious than anyone could ever hope to be.

27

"Don't grieve. Anything you lose
comes round in another form..."
—Rumi

FIRST CLASS WAS CROWDED. Content to find his row empty, he slid into the window seat. Too much on his mind to bother with mindless banter. He looked forward to writing in his journal and being alone.

Tossing his jacket on the adjacent seat, he watched the parade of people entering the plane. A surprising wave of anxiety swept over him. What was really going to happen once he got home? How was he going to write this book? Would anyone on earth ever believe his experiences? Would he be able to capture, in words, the miracle of all he had learned? Breathing deeply, he tried to calm the voices lashing him with what ifs. What if he couldn't find the right publisher? What if the editors thought he was insane? What if they wanted to delete the most important parts?

He exhaled, and thought *growth*. The Quest has just begun, Ethel Goodwoman told him. There will be challenges, obstacles, stone walls. Include them and move on, always reaching for the light. He smiled. "Growth," he said aloud.

A woman's voice startled him. "Excuse me?"

A familiar red-haired beauty stared down at him.

"Catherine? I can't believe it!"

Startled, the woman replied, "You must be mistaken. My name is Elizabeth."

He was speechless. Was this possible? She looked just like Catherine, the same mesmerizing green eyes. "My God..."

"Are you okay?"

He stared, enthralled. Her hair, a gorgeous fiery red, shoulder length, swept back behind her ears where two small emerald studs glittered. Reading glasses hung from an exquisite, beaded chain around her neck. She was dressed elegantly in a creme silk tunic and slacks. Her no-nonsense running shoes made him smile. "Sir," she repeated gently, touching his shoulder. He shivered. "Should I get the flight attendant?"

Covering his mouth, he pretended to cough. "No, I mean, yes I'm fine. I just thought... you look so familiar."

"Mind if I sit? This is my seat." Apologizing, he scrambled to move his jacket. She sat down beside him, pushed back her seat to get comfortable, then opened a worn leather briefcase. Not wanting to stare, he pretended to fumble with his seat belt.

"Funny," she said "My middle name is Catherine." Her smile took his breath away. "You must be psychic."

"Guess so."

Inside the briefcase were thick folders and a laptop. Flipping through color coded files, it looked as though she had packed the entire office. Turning toward him, she asked "Were you here on vacation, Mister...?"

"Allan," he blurted, feeling like an idiot. "Allan Quinn Fitzpatrick."

Awkwardly, he stuck out his hand. She graciously accepted it and he noticed, relieved, that she wore no rings at all.

"So, Mr. Fitzpatrick," she said, slipping her hand from his, "was it a vacation that brought you to Ireland?"

"Uh, well, sort of." He could still feel her warmth in his hand. "Kind of a working vacation."

"Me, too," she said. "I think mine turned out to be more work than vacation."

He relaxed, feeling more at ease with her. "May I ask what kind of work?"

She looked at him again. "Publishing."

"Really? What exactly do you do?

"I'm the executive editor at Sterling Tree Books."

He fell back against the seat. Sterling Tree was an internationally recognized publishing house highly respected by authors. This was beyond any coincidence. He could practically hear Faery singing, *"witness life and praise all things."*

"Hallelujah," he whispered, smiling.

"I beg your pardon?"

He turned and looked at her, deeply. "May I call you Elizabeth?"

She gazed back, noticing his incredible blue eyes. "Certainly," she said, her cheeks flushing with heat.

Drawing closer to her, knowing they would be traveling together far beyond this flight, he began, "Tell me, Elizabeth, how do you feel about the notion of faeries?"

EPILOGUE

THE PLANE DIPPED its wing as the twinkling lights of John F. Kennedy International Airport came into view. Allan excused himself and walked to the back. No one was around. He stretched his arms high above his head and, in one graceful motion, jumped. His palms touched the ceiling of the plane and instantly pushed through, as if the cold steel was softened butter. He hauled himself up, out of the plane's cabin, emerging into silence. It was not the sky. It was not a cloud bank. It was, instead, a bright space, white and empty, white as this very sheet of paper. White as this glowing screen. Without any hesitation, he lifted his eyes and looked, not at the red-haired beauty sitting next to him, or the pilot flying the plane or any other character in this story. He looked at You. Yes, You. You who hold these pages in Your hands. The time has come. Do not be afraid. You are the Chosen One.

And this is what he said:

"Are You willing to accept the Quest?"

ACKNOWLEDGEMENTS

I'M DEEPLY GRATEFUL to everyone who has contributed to bringing Quest into the world. The process has been a wild roller coaster ride—challenging, thrilling, ridiculously scary, and intensely rewarding. And none of it would have happened if it weren't for the wonderful community of men and women who have supported this project. Mahalo nui loa, again and again, to . . . **Travis Weaver,** for your exquisite pen-and-ink illustrations gracing the pages of this story, your immense generosity during that process, all while navigating (literally) life on a sailboat in Mexico with your family. www.travisweaver.org; **Barbara McKell,** for your beautifully and perfectly rendered illustration of the Quest pin. www.barbaramckell.com; **Sheila Smallwood,** for your innate artistry, book design mastery, and our Empowerment friendship. www.sheilasmallwooddesign.com; **Pineniece Joshua,** for your passionate love of words, and for often understanding Allan's journey better than me; **Susan Killeen,** for your open-hearted, wise, and kick-ass copy-editing; **Everett O'Keefe** and your wonderful team at Ignite Press for their incredible publishing expertise; **Jon Christensen,** for your astute feedback and ongoing support; **Mariyah Sultan,** for listening enthusiastically to the entire book during those long drives; **Brenda Ignacio,** for your love and eagerness to spread the word about the first edition;

Lucie Lynch, for always being my personal, leopard-leggings Faery; Dennis Buckingham, for your honest and insightful comments; Alberta Nye, for our sacred Lana'i forest ceremony—you are the true godmother of Quest; Rachel Fergusen, for loving the story from the beginning; Al Aubrey, my opinionated father-in-law who only consumed shoot-em'-up westerns, for reading Quest and then insisting, year after year after year, "you should publish that book!" And my father, Ruby Mager, for your brave and tender heart.

Lastly, the most important cheerleaders of all, two extraordinary men without whom I could not have ever completed any of this. My heart overflows with gratitude to. . .Dennis Aubrey, my devoted husband and life partner, for reading Quest a zillion times, for urging me never to give up, for comforting me during my decades of insecurity and doubt, and for being unafraid—even though you're a meat-eatin' man's man—to openly admit your love of fairies (and Faery). Reyn Aubrey, my courageous, compassionate, visionary son, for believing in this story (and me) and its timeless message. And to Manhattan, especially Central Park, where the trees and bushes consoled me; to that miraculous peapod in East New York, Brooklyn; and finally, to the Hawaiian Islands, especially Lana'i, where Quest was born.

AUTHOR'S NOTES

BEFORE I THANK YOU for taking this journey with me, there's someone who insists on saying a few words.

Congratulations, dearies! You made it this far! Just remember that everyone's Quest looks different, although one thing certainly remains the same: We, all of us—Allan, Faery, and of course yours truly—will be there cheering you on. And no matter what happens, don't give up— at least not for too long—and always, always keep reaching for the sun.

Ta ta,
Ethel G.

P.S. One more thing. Don't forget Faery's sage advice. Words have magic, like flowers, so choose yours with care.

Okay, back to me. I've been playing with words since childhood. My publishing credits include a dozen books, translated into many languages, plus an international bestseller about nature spirits. I'm also a journalist, poet, mixed-media artist, performer, and creativity/book coach. Learn more at www.marciazinamager.com

I appreciate you taking the time to read and reflect on Quest. If you would like to dive even deeper and get your very own Quest pin, please go to my website: marciazinamager.com/quest

"And you? When will you begin that
long journey into yourself?"
—RUMI

Made in the USA
Thornton, CO
01/29/23 17:00:31